AT THE CHIME OF
A CITY CLOCK

A THE CHIME OF A CITY CLOCK

D J Taylor

**WINDSOR
PARAGON**

First published 2010
by Constable
This Large Print edition published 2012
by AudioGO Ltd
by arrangement with
Constable & Robinson Ltd

Hardcover   ISBN: 978 1 4713 1292 2
Softcover   ISBN: 978 1 4713 1293 9

British Library Cataloguing in Publication Data available

Printed and bound in Great Britain by
MPG Books Group Limited

For John Walsh

A city freeze
Get on your knees
Pray for warmth and green paper
A city drought, you're down and out
See your trousers don't taper
Saddle up
Kick your feet
Ride the range of a London street
Travel to a local plane
Turn around and come back again

And at the chime of a city clock
Put up your road block
Hang onto your crown
For a stone in a tin can
Is wealth to a city man
Who leaves his armour down.

NICK DRAKE

CONTENTS

CONTENTS

PART ONE

PART ONE

1

CALEDONIAN ROAD

Wanted: smart lad (18–20) for clerical duties in fur trade, EC2. Good refs essential. £2.10s p.w. & prospects. Apply: Mr Berkmann, Gant & Rosenthal, 17b Finsbury Pavement.

Holborn and Farringdon Gazette, *5 August 1931*

The dawn came up over the Caledonian Road at about six o'clock. At this point, the life of the street—the part of it near His Majesty's Prison Pentonville—that had shown signs of lapsing over the past half-hour began to redouble its pace. The number of cars shuttling back and forth past the mouth of the underground slowly increased. A pair of heavy lorries went by, three-tonners bound for the meat market at Smithfield. A taxi came crawling around the corner of Brewery Road, carrying home a gang of white-faced tarts to furnished rooms in Maida Vale. As one kind of commerce came to an end, others were starting up. The door of a lock-up yard stuck between the sides of two grey-fronted houses opened a yard or so into the street and a costermonger edged into view dragging his empty barrow through the gap. A man in a dirty white apron began to take down the shutters of the cafe thirty yards further away, stacked the shutters in a neat pile next to the doorway and then brought out a chalked blackboard that read: *Teas*: *3d*; *tea and two slices*: *6d*; *kipps*: *6d*. The sun, trapped for the last half-hour behind a giant gasometer that aggrandized over the skyline, came suddenly into view, drenching pavement, road, cars and lorries alike in a harsh orange light. It was about twenty past six.

*   *   *

He woke just as the light began seeping through the space at the bottom of the blind. For some reason he hadn't drawn it down properly the night before. Why was that, he wondered? The window looked out into the road and you always got the early sun. There had been a snatch of dance music playing in his head—Henry Hall? He couldn't remember—and he lay there under the sheet for a moment trying to recapture it, until a little more light seeped in under the blind and the noise of one of the Smithfield lorries jerked him fully awake; this made him look round wildly and take stock of his surroundings. It was a small room, not more than nine feet square, with the bed jammed into the far corner. As well as the bed it contained a wash-hand stand, a cupboard, a wardrobe, a gas-ring and a chair. There was a picture on the wall of Carole Lombard in a bathing dress, which had been cut out of *Film Fun*. His belongings were piled up on the chair, together with his wallet—he had taken the precaution of hiding this under his jacket—his watch and a packet of Player's Weights. Wondering if the girl was awake yet, he slid slowly out from between the covers, balanced himself on the balls of his feet—there was no carpet and he didn't want a splinter in his toe—and began to put on his clothes. He'd got the shirt on—there was a collar tag saying 'T. Harris', rather than his own name, Leo Merman.

4

But the trousers were only halfway up when she rolled over and lay on her side to stare at him.

'What time is it?'

His watch was caught up in the folds of his shirt. 'It's jest gone about half-past six.'

'What's the hurry then?'

'Got an appointment,' he said, a bit importantly, despite himself. 'Down in the City. Got to see a feller.'

He shot her a good steady look as he said this, just to show her that no woman was going to muck him about. Bending down again for his tie, he found that some of her clothes had got mixed up with his and started angrily to separate them. F——g tarts' clothes messing up his good suit! The idea.

'Nice,' she said. She'd found the packet of Player's Weights and had one lit between her fingers. ''Aving a job to go to.' She was about twenty-two, rather pale and dark, and barely covered up by the ochre-coloured sheet.

'Who said anything about having a f——g job?'

He was a bit disconcerted by the girl. Why didn't she get up, like himself, and clear off? Women were always hanging around you, nagging away. If she thought she was coming down into the City with him, she could do the other thing. He had his suit on now. A bit frayed around the elbows maybe, but it would do. In any case, he'd only be there the day, wouldn't he? The girl was still smoking the cigarette, one hand holding the sheet against her chest.

'Ent you going to get me some breakfast?'

He finished pushing the knot of his tie into place and jabbed his thumb towards the window. 'F——g caff over the road.' Seeing the look on her face,

5

he relented slightly. 'Can have a cup of tea 'ere if you want. Why don't you put your clothes on like a good girl and I'll make you a nice cup of tea?'

There was a sink outside in the hall, next to a cane-backed chair where someone had left a brown-paper parcel that smelt of cat meat. As he filled the kettle he whistled softly through his teeth. Get down to Finsbury Pavement by nine. See the feller. Do the business with the key to the Thompson and there you were. When he came back into the room the girl was sitting by the cupboard buttoning up her blouse. He'd met her in a pub in Hoxton where she'd been waiting for her sister to come back from a trip to the Hackney Empire to see Nervo & Knox with her young man. Somehow he didn't believe in the sister or the sister's young man.

'Here y'are,' he said with fake jollity, putting the kettle on the gas-ring. 'Nice cup of ackamaracka in no time.' He wondered if there was any milk. A brief search turned up half a bottle in the cupboard. He didn't know how long it had been there, but it didn't smell too bad.

'This tea tastes funny,' she said, when he had given her the cup. Here in the cold light of morning she seemed less self-possessed. She had a pathetic little cheap handbag—one of those things you could buy in Petticoat Lane for a florin—and he found himself sneering at it. A real cheap little piece, she was.

'So what you doing with yourself this morning?' he asked her. All the time he said it he was looking out of the window at the cars—she'd pulled up the blind while he was out filling the kettle—and considering his route down into the City.

6

'I don't know. I might go and see my friend in Kensington.'

He wondered whether the friend in Kensington was a tart or one of those girls who couldn't decide what they were. He'd known plenty of them. He drank another swallow of tea—it was vile stuff, the colour of burnt umber—and thought again about the route down to Finsbury Pavement. Get on to the Farringdon Road. Then left along Old Street. Take a right along the City Road, and there you were. All this time he'd barely registered the girl's presence, but there she was staring at him again.

'I'll see you back here then, shall I?' she said, almost shyly. 'Later on.'

'Can't do that,' he said, improvising rapidly. 'This ain't my place you see. Borrowed it off a mate. Tell you what,' he went on, blinking furiously, 'meet me at six. Liverpool Street. Under the clock. Know it?'

'Course I know it.'

'Right then. Six o'clock.' Come six o'clock he'd be with the Bloke, getting his twenty quid. And he wouldn't be coming back here. No sir. Looking at his watch he saw it was nearly 7 a.m.. The sun burned suddenly against the curtain-less window and he held up his hand to shield his face. Get the key to the Thompson, whip out the box of tricks and there you were. No trouble.

'Seven o'clock,' he said decisively. 'Can't hang around here drinking f——g tea. You getting the bus down to your friend in Kensington?'

'S'pose I might.'

'You'll be needing your fare then.'

He saw by the look on her face that she'd counted on him giving her more than the bus fare. Half a quid maybe. Well, she could whistle for that.

He could feel the frayed patches on his suit rubbing against his elbows. Christ! What if they found him out? 'So long,' he said, as they stood together on the steps of the house.

'So long.'

If he had looked back, he would have seen her walk off not in the direction of the bus stop but away east towards Barnsbury. Only he didn't look back. Instead he plunged south, past the lines of stationary cars and the cafe with its teas and two slices. F——g teas and two slices, he told himself as he went by. He'd have a steak tonight, after this caper was over. He hurried on, thinking of the office in Finsbury Pavement, the twenty quid the Bloke was going to give him that night, and the man whose identity he was about to make his own.

2

RED HAIR, BLACK SWEATER

Sound Advice for the Salesman: I. Initiative

Remember! The salesman's task is to sell himself as well as the product in his demonstration bag. When you have 'made a sale' to a satisfied customer, you may congratulate yourself that this individual has responded to your personality. Even the finest products cannot sell themselves! No, they need your enthusiasm, your recommendation, your reassurance. So use your initiative! Look closely at the situations in which you find yourself and make them work to your advantage. If the customer has a particular susceptibility, play on it! If the customer expresses a particular preference, try to match his request. And remember, the customer who refuses your product is also refusing you!

Abraxas Salesman's Handbook

Fact is, Susie and me getting together was the queerest thing. It was all because of the Cep.

That was what we used to call the demonstrations, seeing that 'Customer Exposition Programme' was a bit of a mouthful. Only someone who reckoned on making supervisor said that. Everyone else made do with 'Cep'.

It happened this way. By that stage of the summer I was pretty much on my uppers. I'd sold a couple of stories, but one of the magazines had stopped paying and the other wrote to say that they couldn't fit it in until Christmas. It was the slump, everyone said. Plus I'd had a run-in with Mrs Fanshawe, the landlady at my digs. There was money owing, too, at the laundry and half-a-dozen other places. Anyhow, I got talking to this chap I met at the Labour round the back of Shaftesbury Avenue and he said there was a firm in Holborn looking for door-to-doors. 'Commission job is it?' I asked—I'd done door-to-doors before and got used to the tricks—but he said no, there was a basic of two quid a week. That bucked me up, because two quid went a long way, even at Mrs Fanshawe's, and I was halfway to Holborn before I remembered that I hadn't asked him what it was that I'd be selling.

Turned out the firm had an office in Doughty Street—the last place you'd expect to find a door-to-door merchant—and pretty soon I was parked in one of those rooms that are full of tubular chairs and gunmetal filing cabinets, being interviewed by a red-nosed character named Roper, who clearly drank like a fish and had pretty obviously seen better days. 'Got any experience of this kind of work?' he asked, and I said yes, as it happened, I'd sold vacuum cleaners down on the south coast, Bognor way. 'Well then,' he said, 'you shouldn't have any trouble with this', and he reached into a cupboard next to the desk and pulled out what looked like a double-sized milk bottle filled with some sort of pinkish liquid. 'Carpet cleaning lotion,' he said. 'You spread it over the floor, wait a minute or two for it to dry and then clear it off with a brush and pan. You'd be surprised what comes up.'

10

There were some old pieces of carpet on a side table and he told me to have a go, so I shook the bottle in what I hoped was a professional-looking manner—it was thick, runny stuff, like a milkshake—decanted it over the carpet and then brushed away like billy-oh. It seemed to do the trick, so Roper said he'd give me a fortnight's trial: twenty-five bob a week basic—the chap at the Labour had been talking through his hat—and a thirty-three per cent commission. The stuff was seven-and-six a bottle, which worked out at half-a-crown a time. There was even a sub—five bob—to pay for bus fares to my beat, which was up Kensal Green way somewhere.

'We never got subs down in Bognor,' I said.

'Salesman's graveyard, that is,' Roper told me. I couldn't tell if his hand was shaking or not.

So what with the job, and the five bob in hand, and the hot weather keeping up, I was in a pretty forgiving mood as I sailed up the Harrow Road on a bus with half-a-dozen bottles of the lotion clinking in the big canvas carry-bag Roper had given me. On the way I read the salesman's handbook he'd shown me, which was all about calling the customer 'madam' and wiping your feet on the mat, along with some scientific stuff about what went into the lotion and what to do if it got on your skin by mistake. It was gone twelve by the time I arrived at Kensal Green and half of me was voting for a quick one and a cheese sandwich out of the five bob, but I'd been on the door-to-door before and I knew that the lunch hour is a good time for finding people in.

And that's when the trouble started. I tried a dozen doors before one would even open, and

11

another dozen before I could so much as get the lotion out of the case. One old lady did invite me into her parlour, but it turned out that this was because she wanted to tell someone about her Sealyham dying. Another one got the idea that I was a Jehovah's Witness and started telling me about her aunt who was communicating with her from the Other Side, where she was the high priestess of a tribe of natives in the Amazonian rainforest. Finally I lugged the case up the path of what looked like a boarding house—there were six or seven bells on the door, and someone had left that morning's *Mirror* on the mat—and pressed the bottom bell, thinking that if this one didn't work I really would go and have a quick one and a cheese sandwich in the pub I could see across the way.

'Yes?'

She must have been in her mid twenties, red-haired and wearing a black jumper that was a size too small—several sizes if you asked me. A real looker, in other words, and not what you usually found in Kensal Green on a Tuesday lunchtime.

'Good afternoon, madam. Wonderful late-summer weather we're having.'

'Yes, I suppose we are rather.' Then she clammed up, leaving me desperately trying to remember what the book said you should do next.

'Did you know, madam, that over the course of a year the average domestic carpet accumulates more than 3lbs of dirt?'

'Gracious! That sounds a lot.'

'Dirt that has a uniquely detrimental effect on the carpet's fibres. In fact, scientific studies have shown that nearly half of all carpets are affected by a mould-carrying fungus caused by dirt.'

12

I had her full attention now and time to appreciate that the red hair and the tight jumper weren't a false card: she really was a looker and no mistake.

'Is that what you're selling? Carpets, I mean.'

'No, madam. I represent the Abraxas Carpet Cleaning Company. Abraxas', I extemporized cheerfully, 'was the Greek god of cleanliness and hygiene. Our products are guaranteed to eliminate dirt in a fraction of the time demanded by conventional cleaning methods.'

'You'd better come in,' she said.

The scheme, as set down by old Roper, or whoever had written the handbook, was that you gave them a trial out of the demonstration flask, the theory being that they'd be so impressed you could then sell them a full bottle on the spot. As she led me through a shadowy hallway in the direction of what looked like the parlour I thought a bit more science wouldn't go amiss, so I said: 'In addition to which they contain both physostocine and araldite, which chemists acknowledge offer the best means of maintaining carpet fibre in its optimal state.'

Oddly enough, the parlour was like the old lady's, which is to say that there were two or three photographs from the last century lying on top of a mahogany sideboard, a framed certificate stating that John Smith had been elected Primo Buffo in the Royal Antediluvian Order of Buffaloes and a view of a melancholy garden fenced off from the rest of civilization by three towering brick walls. Anyway, I'd got out the demonstration flask and was shaking it about—you weren't supposed to use more than a couple of capfuls but I figured I ought to make a good impression—when she said:

13

'Is this your regular job?'

'No,' I said, shaking away and giving the carpet a poke with a kind of wire toothbrush Roper had issued me with.

'What do you really do then?'

'I'm a writer,' I said proudly. In my experience you have to be careful telling women you're a writer, but this one seemed to like it because she instantly asked:

'Who do you write for?'

'Last month I had a story in the *New English Review*.'

It was the truth, as well.

'And what name do you write under?'

'James Ross,' I replied.

And lo and behold if she didn't shoot off out of the parlour with the contents of the tight jumper going everywhere, leaving me to grub up more of the dirt from the carpet. A precious lot there was of it, too. When she came back there was a copy of the *New English Review* under her arm and her face had gone crimson.

'You're James Ross,' she said.

'I told you I was.'

'You wrote the story about the dying prostitute.'

It was too good a chance to miss, so I put the demonstration bottle back in the bag and said: 'If you like writers you ought to come to the Wheatsheaf in Rathbone Place on a Thursday night.'

'Thank you,' she said, looking like the girl in the toothpaste advert. 'I'd like that.'

Something struck me and I asked: 'What about the lotion?'

'Oh, it's not my house I'm afraid. You'd have

14

to speak to Mrs Farrell. She's out this afternoon, visiting her sister in Leyton.'

'Never mind,' I said. 'Thursday night at the Wheatsheaf. About eight.'

I was so bucked, what with the date and the *New English Review*, that I was halfway down the street before I realized that I didn't even know her name.

* * *

After that I calmed down a bit, had a sandwich in a Lite-A-Bite bar near Kensal Green tube and got down to some serious selling. The trick, I found— it had been the same with the vacuum cleaners— was to cough a bit and tap your chest while you did the Cep. Then, if anyone looked sympathetic, you murmured something about mustard gas. Luckily I was just old enough to make it look as though I'd fought in the war rather than steaming open envelopes in a hut on the downs at Southern Command. Anyhow, by four-thirty I'd sold three bottles of the stuff and I figured that was enough to be going on with. Besides, the smell, once you'd done five or six Ceps, was something fearful.

By the time I got back to Holborn, Roper had disappeared. Instead there was a long, lugubrious article called Hastings, who smoked Gold Flake so ravenously that he lit the next one off the stub of the one before. He was leery of me at first, but brightened up no end when he heard I'd made a sale.

'Twenty-two and six,' he said. 'Not bad for a first afternoon. Want me to take off the sub now?'

I said no, I'd wait till the end of the week and see how I went, so he took a cash-box off the shelf and palmed me three half-crowns.

'Have a fag?'

'Don't mind if I do.'

They were Woodbines, of course, out of another packet he had in his desk drawer, but I didn't care: I'd been in the game long enough to know that a fag's a fag. Anyhow, he was friendly enough and took me down to a kind of canteen they had in the basement, where some of the other salesmen sat swilling tea out of chipped china mugs and eating stale rock-buns. There were about five of them, all on the wrong side of forty, with wives and kids hanging round their necks fit to drown them, but curiously one was a chap I knew from the vacuum cleaner lark. Ernie Callender, he was called, and he was famous for giving the eye to the supervisor's wife.

'So,' he said, when he'd fixed me up with a cup of tea and another cig, 'still on the selling game, I see. What beat did they give you?'

'Kensal Green.'

Callender whistled through the gaps in his teeth. He was one of those tall, thin characters who look as though they ought to be playing the gravedigger in *Hamlet*. 'Regular undertaker's parlour that is, boy. You ought to be down in Notting Hill with me. Eight, ten bottles a morning I'm saying goodbye to there. Look, that Hastings is a decent bloke. Let me see if I can fix it.'

'Thanks very much,' I said.

He went off for a bit after that, leaving me in the basement with a couple of poor old dug-outs who talked about their livers and their wives' mothers, and I thought about Susie, although I didn't yet know her name, and wondered if my luck

16

mightn't be changing at last. What I should have remembered was that Callender, as well as carrying on with the supervisors' wives, had always been a great one for a fiddle. But you see, I've always been the trusting sort and I swear the thought never occurred to me.

*　　　*　　　*

When I got back to my digs there was a letter from my old lady propped up against the door, so I took it inside and read it lying on the bed while the kettle boiled. The old lady didn't write often, and when she did it was the same thing: the wretched Cairn terriers that fouled up the house, the people she played bridge with and the state of the drains. This time was no exception. Apparently, one of the dogs had died after overeating and one of the bridge partners had distinguished herself by revoking three times in the space of half-an-hour. I had some Basildon Bond notepaper that Netta had given to me when we were still speaking to each other, and after a bit I hauled it down from the shelf, unscrewed the top of the gold-nibbed fountain pen I used to write with, and wrote:

Darling Mums,
*   It was very good to hear from you: I was wondering how you were getting on. Life here is very quiet. I have given up the insurance job as I found that it was not suited to my tastes and capabilities. Also the people were not quite. Happily an opening has presented itself in the marine underwriting business, which I intend enthusiastically to pursue. I have been to several*

17

exhibitions and taken in one or two shows. The last Cochran was particularly good—perhaps you will have read about it in the Morning Post? *I hope to write again soon with news of my engagement. She is called Hermione Kyslant— the shipping people, as you doubtless know.*

> *Best love,*
> *James*
> *P.S. Work is exceedingly busy, but I hope to motor down and visit you soon.*

I always wrote to the old lady like this, not because it was true but because it was the kind of thing she liked to hear. As for motoring down and visiting her soon, well I didn't have a car and I hadn't set eyes on her in two years.

After I'd nipped out to catch the last post and turned over five bob out of the seven-and-six to Mrs Fanshawe, who was cooking a haddock down in her basement, I lay on the bed again with my hands round the back of my neck and read an old copy of *Police News* that I found pressed between the mattress and the wall, but it was a year old and most of the murders had been solved. Then I thought about Susie and whether or not she'd mind being brought back here, and what she'd look like minus the jumper. That was the kind of thing I used to think about in those days, along with God, and whether or not he existed, and if he did whether he liked me, which I always thought improbable.

3

FINSBURY PAVEMENT

*The wayfarer wending his path southward to
the City's dark, enraptured heart will chance
upon many a locale that not the most barnacled
advocate of the pleasures of 'Old London' could
consider picturesque. We have lingered long
in Clerkenwell. We have taken our pleasures
in Hoxton. We have heard good reports even
of Somers Town. But Finsbury Pavement,
alas, holds scant attraction for a traveller in
metropolitan romance, being noisy, modern,
polyglot, furious and clerical . . .*

H.V. Morton, City Haunts and Homes *(1931)*

On the far side of Finsbury Pavement, jammed
between a row of shops and the City Gas and Coke
Company, there were a pair of houses that some
enterprising landlord had divided up into offices.
Seeing that one of the polished brass plates said
Gant & Rosenthal: Furriers, he crossed over the road
and went and smoked a cigarette under an awning.
Only 8.30 a.m.: plenty of time to take a look-see.
That was the idea. The girl, who had vanished
completely from his consciousness during the last
ninety minutes, had now wandered back into it and,
as he lounged under the awning with the smoke
rising in a little cloud over his head, he considered
her points. Now he came to think about it, he hadn't
had a bad time. For a moment he saw her legs again,

19

moving under his in the bed. Perhaps he ought to go and meet her under the clock at Liverpool Street at six. But that would mean missing the Bloke and risking the twenty quid. Women!

The first group of office workers was streaming down the pavement, disgorged from buses or come from the tube at Moorgate, and he stared at them keenly, trying to work out which among them might be employed by Gant & Rosenthal, the furriers. That meant skins, didn't it, fur coats and such? Perhaps, if the going got good, he'd help himself to a fur coat. A borassic'd do anything for a fur coat. A tall girl in a cloche hat turned into the doorway of the building where the Gant & Rosenthal plate hung and he hoped that she worked there. After all, he'd need something to look at while he was biding his time, wouldn't he? In this way another five minutes passed. A wind blew up across the pavement and sent the old newspapers and the bits of rubbish at his feet into a little whirling tornado. He looked at it sombrely. There were clouds coming in from the north: if he stayed here much longer he'd catch it. To his surprise he found his courage had deserted him. *Easy as pie* the Bloke had said. *Chap who did the hiring's gone on holiday. Bloke he gave the job to's been warned off. So you're him. Easy as pie.* But what if it wasn't? What if the chap who did the hiring had decided not to go on holiday after all? It was two minutes to nine now. Anyway, if it came to it he could just say there was some mistake, or even leg it. He'd done that before. Throwing down the cigarette stub, he crossed back over the road to the doorway.

Gant & Rosenthal were on the first floor. You could smell the fur halfway up the stairs. A kind

20

of heavy, musty scent, like those old Bradys on the tubes. On the landing he met a fat, balding man in a serge suit who was flipping through a pile of letters with plump fingers like saveloy sausages.

'Help you son?'

Not a gent, then. That was a relief. He had a feeling that a gent might see through him. A whole lot less chance of pulling the old amarakadiver with a gent. There were names crowding into his head. The bloke who was supposed to have hired him; the bloke who was the other bloke's boss.

'You Mr Rosenthal?' he asked, with an effort.

'That's right.'

'Well I'm glad of that,' he said. 'Only Mr Berkmann told me to ask for you.' Now he was spinning the spiel, it didn't sound so bad. 'On account of I'm supposed to be working here. You see my name's'—he thought he was going to falter, but didn't—'Stanley Dunn.'

The fat man was still looking idly at the letters. A shonk too: always tell that from the size of their beaks. Probably had some borassic stashed away in one of those houses up in Golders Green. 'Dunn?' he said. 'You'll be the new clurk, then?'

'That's right, sir. Mr Berkmann told me to come here at nine o'clock this morning. Said he'd . . .'

'Yuss, yuss, I know all about it.' Mr Rosenthal was so transparently not a gent that it was comical to see. 'Mr Berkmann's gone off on holiday. Fortnight in Herne Bay. But that don't make no difference. You better step in here. Come far this morning?'

'Caledonian Road.'

'That's funny.' Mr Rosenthal was pushing his way through a large, glass partition door. Beyond lay a workroom with a couple of stools and a long plasterboard table from which a vast pile of furs extended almost to the ceiling. 'Could've sworn your letter said you lived in Walthamstow.'

Christ! The Bloke hadn't said anything about living in f——g Walthamstow. 'Bin staying at my uncle's house,' he said meekly. 'On account of it being his birthday on Sunday and having all the family round.' The smell of the furs was quite overpowering: enticing but sickly sweet.

'Yuss, yuss,' Mr Rosenthal muttered. 'Well, just as long as you get here on time I don't care if you're coming from Buckingham Palace in a coach and pair. Now then, you sit down there'—he pointed to a third stool, out of range of the plasterboard table—'and I daresay Miss Tozer will come and get you started. I b'lieve she's powdering her nose just at the moment.'

He went and sat on the stool, crossing one leg over the other so that the bottom of his trousers rode up slightly above the ankle. Christ! He'd only forgotten to put his socks on, hadn't he? Sitting there with his arms folded and the furs banked up on either side of him—the sunlight coming through the window rippled off the glass surface in a myriad of tiny sheens—he had a queer sensation of being deep underground, down in some terrible cavern at the earth's core. Mr Rosenthal had taken off his coat, which he hung on a rickety coat stand, and was proceeding into a glass-fronted cubicle at the back of the room. There was a noise of footsteps coming up the stairs. Outside a clock was chiming the hour.

*   *   *

He was torn out of his reverie by the clock striking again. He listened attentively as the first stroke faded away, but there was nothing more. One o'clock, eh? That made four hours he'd been sitting here with his ankles carefully concealed by the folds of his trouser-legs so that no one should see he wasn't wearing socks. In that time, he calculated, he'd left the stool twice—once to visit the lavatory, another time to see Mr Rosenthal in his office. Four hours! It was surprising how much you could find out about a place in that time. He knew, for example, that in addition to himself, Gant & Rosenthal had four employees: Mr Rosenthal himself, Miss Tozer, who typed Mr Rosenthal's letters and made telephone calls to transport firms, Mr Berkmann, the office manager, who was on holiday in Herne Bay, and Gregory the office boy. There were also a couple of travelling representatives, but they were not often seen on the premises, Miss Tozer had said. The Thompson was in Mr Rosenthal's office and the key to it—though he couldn't be absolutely sure of this—was in the drawer of his desk. Well he'd have that, wouldn't he? The question was: how? His mouth gaped a little and he settled himself again on the stool and tried to read some more of Gant & Rosenthal's catalogue, which Mr Rosenthal had told him to get acquainted with sharpish. *Chinchilla. Sealskin. Mink.* There was a picture of a borassic wearing a fox fur that lay invitingly over her shoulders and he winked at it.

'Didn't you bring any sandwiches or anything for your lunch?' Miss Tozer wondered from the adjoining stool.

Miss Tozer was the tall girl in the cloche hat he'd seen in the vestibule. She would have been about twenty-five, he thought, with a nice smile but a terrible suet-pudding complexion, and she was disposed to be friendly.

'Ain't hungry,' he said. Seeing he had a receptive audience, he went on: 'It's a funny thing about me, you know, but I never get hungry at lunchtime. Never could get anything down. Not even when I was a kid.'

There were only the two of them there, Gregory having been sent on an errand to the freight office at Liverpool Street, and Mr Rosenthal having departed to lunch. Patting the right-hand pocket of his suit, and being reassured by the clink of the tin concealed in it, he decided to chance his luck a bit further.

'Here,' he said. 'I don't suppose you're going out at all.'

'Well . . .' Miss Tozer said, 'I don't know that I am.'

'Only it's like this,' he said. 'I can't go myself, cos it's my first day and Mr Rosenthal's told me to read this catalogue. But if you were going out I'd take it kindly if you'd get me a copy of *Boxing News*.'

He could tell at once that he'd said the right thing. 'Do you like boxing?' Miss Tozer asked. Christ! If her face didn't look exactly like a jam roly-poly.

'That's right.'

'My sister and I went to a boxing match once,' Miss Tozer said reminiscently. 'At Ealing town hall. There was a boy got hit on the nose and bled something shocking. All over the floor. And my sister felt faint and had to go outside.'

24

'I've bin hit a few times myself,' he admitted.

'You'll have to answer the telephone while I'm out,' she said. 'If it's the freight company from Manchester, Mr Rosenthal wants to know what happened to the parcel we sent to Sheffield last week.'

'You're a good sort,' he said.

Alone in the workroom, with the piles of furs banked up on either side of him and the sound of Miss Tozer's footsteps tripping away down the stairs, he felt a little stab of triumph. It wasn't always so easy, working the old amarakadiver. He had the tin out of his pocket by now and down on the workbench, so that he could see the green layer of wax gleaming up from within. All he needed now was the key. The key! Mr Rosenthal's office, in which he found himself a second or two later, merely disgusted him. A gent would have had one of those long, roll-top desks that you saw in the films, not this flimsy contrivance with a cheap veneer. There was a tear-off calendar on the wall, with the compliments of Messrs Gargery & Lowenstein, freight hauliers, printed on it, and he saw that it was three days behind. F——g old yid, not even keeping his calendar up to date. The key. Where was it? The first two he found in the desk drawer were too big—he could tell that without trying them. No good putting them in the Thompson. But the third was smaller, and with a particular groove in the cut.

He held it up to the light for a bit and looked at it. Yes, that was the one. He stared out through the glass partition again and then twisted round to face the Thompson with the key jabbing out of his fingers. That was it. He could feel the lock turning under his hand. For a moment he wondered about pulling it open and taking a look inside, but instinct warned him off. If Rosenthal came back and the money was gone, he'd know who'd taken it. Almost reverently, he held the key between the fingers and thumb of his right hand, laid the tin open in the palm of his left and pressed the key down a quarter of an inch into the surface of the wax. Drawing it out again, he looked critically at the impression it left and then pressed it down a second time. Then he sealed up the tin and put it back in his pocket. All done. Except—whew! Look at that, would you—a strand or two of the wax hung off the edges of the key. Give him away like a whore in a church that would. Carefully he took a handkerchief out of his pocket and burnished the key until no trace of the wax remained. That was the mulligatawny!

Five minutes later, when Miss Tozer returned from her excursion with a copy of *Boxing News* under her arm, he was sitting on his stool with the catalogue laid out before him on the workbench.

*　　*　　*

There was a clock striking six as he came down Old Street and turned right into the City Road. He slowed his pace and listened to it above the noise of the traffic, the click of the women's heels and the cries of the newspaper sellers. The tin rattled in his suit pocket as he went along. A policeman standing in a shop doorway stared neutrally at him as he came into the City Road and he glared angrily back. The way the coppers looked at you always annoyed him. The steps leading down into the Bloke's basement beneath the Jew tailor and the Kwik-fit Razor Co. were strewn with orange peel and he kicked it aside with the tip of his boot. Images of the day that had passed ran through his head. Mr Rosenthal had come back to the office at half-past three smelling of brandy and had fallen asleep at his desk. Miss Tozer had asked him what he'd thought of Maxie Schmelling. He didn't mind Miss Tozer, for all her suet-pudding face. Borassics like that you could do what you liked with and they never seemed to mind. If he'd asked Miss Tozer for a date she'd have lapped him up. It didn't take a Sexton Blake to see that. Catch *him* going with *that* ugly mug, though! He wondered what they'd say—her and Mr Rosenthal and Gregory the office boy—when he didn't show next morning. And the box-file full of orders Mr Rosenthal had got out for him lying ready on the workbench, too!

The Bloke's basement was aquarium-dim, even though the electric light was on. There was a packing case split open on the floor and the Bloke's secretary was gathering up her things at the desk. The Bloke stood a little way off, inspecting what looked like a plaster cast that had clearly just come out of the packing case.

'Look,' said the Bloke's secretary. 'Here's Leo come to see you.' If he'd have been the Bloke he'd have kept the secretary behind for a little extra dictation, no question, but the Bloke never seemed to take any notice of her. He just said: 'Thank you, Miss Chamberlain', and they watched her as she slung her bag under her arm and went off up the steps with the contents of her jersey rolling about like a pair of coconuts in a sack.

'Nice girl,' he said, remembering the missed appointment at Liverpool Street. Never mind.

27

There were ways of fixing that.

'I'm sure you're right,' the Bloke said. He'd never worked out whether the Bloke was a gent or not, for all the morning coat and the striped trousers. He had a feeling gents didn't park themselves in basements on the City Road. But you could never tell. 'Well now, how are you Leo?'

'So-so, I reckon.'

'Clerical life suits you, does it?'

'Don't fancy it much.' He had the tin in his hand now. 'Wonder how them clerks puts up with it.'

'How they put up with it?' The Bloke seemed delighted with this. He extended his fingers and touched the tin. 'What sort of a place?'

'Door leads in from the street. 'Nother door for the office. F——g glass partitions. Thompson's on the shelf.'

'I'm very much obliged to you,' the Bloke said. He ran the fingers of the hand that wasn't holding the tin through his sandy hair. 'Truly. You'll want this, I daresay?'

'Too right, I want it.'

He was down on the platform at the underground—there was still some faint thought in his head that he might make his way to Liverpool Street—before he remembered to look in the envelope. Inside it were two five-pound notes. He held it open and shook it out carefully, but nothing else emerged. Ten pounds! Twenty, the Bloke had promised. He could remember him saying it at that place in Soho where the nancy boy had nearly upset a drink over his coat. Five minutes later he was back at the bottom of the steps, where there seemed to be even more orange peel than before, but the office was locked up and the light behind

28

the grey window more aquarium-like than ever. He kicked the door a couple of times, but it was shut fast. The f——r! Cheating him out of his tenner! He stood for a moment or two on the steps, sniffing the air, and then went back up to the City Road, took a few steps eastward on to a pavement wedged with costers' barrows and perambulating women and then disappeared into the crowded streets beyond.

4

A DAY IN THE LIFE

Sound Advice for the Salesman: II. Patience

Every salesman will have a colleague who seems born to the job, who constantly excites the admiration of his fellows by the size of his order book. Remember! Even the very best salesmen are not infallible. There will be times when, through no fault of your own, and despite all your best efforts, the customer will be unresponsive, telling you that she 'isn't interested' or 'has something else to do.' These situations are a test of the salesman's patience and an encouragement to strengthen his resolve. The best salesman is the man who, at any rate, 'comes away with something'—an invitation to call at some future time or an introduction to a third party. You will find that perseverance is your first step on the path to success.

Abraxas Salesman's Handbook

Oddly enough, it was on the Thursday I was due to meet Susie at the Wheatsheaf that things started to go wrong.

First there was a letter from the *Adelphi* saying they couldn't see their way to printing my story for another three months. Then, sidling downstairs with my shoes in my hand in the hope that Mrs Fanshawe wouldn't hear me, I found a note propped up against the door telling me the bill amounted to £6.13s.2d and that 'steps might have to be taken.' Finally, on the bus into town—Ma Fanshawe's digs were Paddington way—I remembered that I'd agreed to meet Callender at the Lyons in High Holborn so we could 'plan our day'. Thinking about this as the bus limped down the Tottenham Court Road—it was one of those dark, grey mornings in late summer with the sun hemmed in by clouds—I turned gloomier still. I hadn't got on too badly with Callender when we were selling vacuum cleaners on the coast, but I was terrified he'd have cooked up some stunt I couldn't decently get myself out of.

And so it turned out. He was sitting in the window of the Lyons when I got there, reading a copy of the *Racing Post*—Callender always backed half-a-dozen second favourites every morning—and when he saw me he shot me one of those knowing little glances that made me think I'd be better off leaving him and his ugly mug down among the cruet bottles and the nippies yelling orders for teas and two slices. Sure enough, as soon as I sat down, he said: 'Doing OK are you this week, Jim?' Fact was, I hadn't been doing too badly, even in Kensal Green: I'd turned five-bob profit the previous day and seven-and-six the day before that. By rights some of this should have gone to Mrs Fanshawe, but I was saving it up, you see, against the night out with Susie. 'Not so bad,' I said. 'Could do with a bit more, though.' And I explained about Ma Fanshawe's £6.13s.2d and the steps that might have to be taken.

Callender listened attentively to all this while he pulled on a Woodbine and made crosses with

31

a pen next to his second favourites. It was then I noticed that as well as the bottle bag they'd issued us with he had an extra parcel full of what looked like bottles of milk. While I was wondering why he needed half a gallon of pasteurised to go out selling carpet lotion, he said: 'I had a word with Hastings. He owes me a favour and he reckoned you could come on the City round with me today.'

'City round?' I said, quite interested despite the fact that Callender was clearly up to something. 'What's that then?'

'Commercial premises,' Callender replied. 'Laundries. Display rooms. I made three quid in Fenchurch Street the other day.'

'Three quid!' I said, sounding a bit surprised, because three quid was about twice as much as a door-to-door could expect if he worked from dawn to dusk.

'That's right.' He gave me a wink that made my heart sink into my boots. 'Here's how you do it. Look.'

There were six pints of milk in the sack, it turned out, bought that morning from Express Dairy by the look of them, and some empty lotion bottles besides. 'Half and half,' Callender went on. 'Strong stuff, that lotion. Mix it up with milk and no one's any the wiser. Double your money and who's to know?' It was a brilliant idea when you thought about it, so brilliant that something told me there had to be a catch.

'Does it still work, though, when you dilute it?' I asked.

'Like I said, strong stuff, that lotion,' Callender said. 'You have to scrub a bit harder with the perishing brush, but I didn't get no complaints.'

32

Well, it seemed all right to me. But then at that particular time anything would have: I was still thinking of Susie and the black jumper. Other chaps aren't like that with women, I've discovered. They can stick them in compartments and bring them out when the moment's right. With me, though, they jump up just when I least expect it. It had been like that with Netta. Anyway, we stopped in at the office for my bottle bag, had a word with a couple of the deadbeats who were hanging round the door—Callender got an envious look or two, I noticed—and then headed off east towards the City. This seemed as good a time as any to renew my acquaintance with Callender, but he was about as non-committal as Ma Fanshawe if you asked her for a week's grace with the rent, and I never did find out what he'd been up to since the owner of the vacuum cleaner firm found him helping his wife with some interior decorating. By this time the rain had come on—there were City gents in morning suits peering out of doorways and then going back for umbrellas—and I didn't fancy our chances much, but Callender was all for it. I think he thought he'd signed up to the three quid a day for life—and so we set off along Cornhill, him doing the south side, me taking the north.

As I'd suspected, it was a frost. Half the places we called at were offices where they made a point of refusing to see door-to-doors; the other half were showrooms of some kind, where as soon as you opened your mouth the manager would duck away to see to a customer. I don't blame them: I'd have done the same. I managed a couple of Ceps in a jeweller's shop and an insurance agent's, but no one was buying and in the end I crossed back over the road, thinking I'd ask Callender if we couldn't move off to an easier beat. He was standing outside a kind of entrance hall where a door led into a laundry and a flight of stairs next to it went off to the offices on the upper floor. 'Go on,' Callender prodded—he hadn't made any sales either, but the thought of the three quid was still goading him on—'I'll try the laundry. You nip upstairs.' I could already see the TO LET sign at the top of the stairwell, though, so I went next door, which was another jeweller's—a big one—and practically got booted out into the street. The place beyond that looked more promising, though—one of those confectioner-cum-tobacconists with dusty packets of Gold Flake in the window and little piles of boiled sweets laid out on trays. It was empty, too, with just the face of the bloke tending the counter visible through the glass, so I picked up my bag and marched in over a carpet that could have taken a bucketful of the lotion, it was so filthy.

'Good morning, sir,' I said, in a voice fit to wake the dead. 'I represent the Abraxas Carpet Cleaning Company. Abraxas, as I'm sure you'll know, was the Greek god of purity. Are you aware that the average household carpet accumulates 3lbs of dust, grit and other substances in each six months of its existence?'

He was a little chap with brindled hair and the most mournful expression I'd ever seen. When I'd finished my piece, he said:

'It's a good job you came in just now, young man.'

'Why's that?' I asked.

'Because if you hadn't I was going to step round the back—there's a ladder there and some rope—

34

and hang myself.'

'I shouldn't do that,' I said, a bit nonplussed. He didn't say anything back, so I carried on: 'I'm sure you've got a lot to live for.' Actually you met this type a lot on the door-to-door. One bloke I knew on the vacuum cleaners had a woman put her head in the gas oven while he was setting up in the next room.

'That's where you're wrong,' he said. 'For two pins I'd do it now, just to give my brother-in-law the aggravation of having to sell the shop.'

'What's the matter with your brother-in-law then?'

'I don't know. I just never did like him, I suppose.'

'Look,' I said. 'Why not let me give you a demonstration of how this stuff works? It might take your mind off things.'

'Well, perhaps it might,' he agreed. 'I don't have to pay for a demonstration, do I?'

'Not a penny,' I told him, trying to call up a sentence I'd memorized from the salesman's handbook. 'It is a pleasure for us merely to give you an idea of what our product can achieve.'

'All right then.'

He seemed to have cheered up, so I got out my Ceps bottle and the wire brush and scrubbed away with a will, while he stood there watching. 'See?' I said after a bit. 'Look how it's bringing back the colour.' It was, too. The patch I'd worked on looked beige rather than lamp-black. While I worked I looked round the shop, which had one of those Abdulla ads with the Bright Young People all standing goofily on someone's doorstep: I'd happily have up-ended a bottle of the lotion all over them.

'You're right,' the little chap said. 'It does work. Tell you what, give me a bottle.'

'They're seven-and-six,' I said.

He took three florins, a shilling and a sixpence out of the till. 'Go on then.'

Before we'd set out, Callender and I had mixed up two of our lotion bottles with equal amounts of milk. I pulled one of these out of the bag and started pouring big dollops of the stuff on to the carpet. 'Hang on,' the little bloke said, 'that don't look right at all.' It didn't, either. It was all kind of syrupy and coagulated, like wallpaper paste, and it stank to high heaven.

'That's all right,' I said. 'With large amounts it takes a moment or two to settle.' Trying to keep his attention away from the carpet, I went on: 'Why was it that you wanted to kill yourself anyway?' He thought about this while I gave the pink syrup a bit of a stir with my brush. It didn't seem to be sinking into the carpet. On the other hand, I couldn't dislodge it from the surface. Finally he said:

'Oh, I don't know. Tired of life, I suppose. Here, that don't look right at all.' The lotion, I now discovered, was forming a kind of crust. When I gave it a prod with the brush a piece of carpet came away.

'If you'll excuse me, sir,' I remarked casually, 'I should just like to consult a colleague of mine who's working a couple of doors down.'

Outside in the street I looked wildly for Callender, but there was no sign. A City gent going by in a bowler hat gave me a look and I realized I was still holding the bottle of lotion in one hand. Then I saw Callender outside the door of the laundry. 'The wretched stuff's all gone wrong,' I

36

yelled. 'I can't get it off the bloody carpet.'

'It was all right yesterday,' Callender said. 'Let's have a dekko.'

Back in the tobacconist's shop the mixture had gone rock hard, like concrete. We stood over it like a couple of farmers examining a dead sheep. The little chap didn't seem particularly fussed. 'I could make you a cup of tea while you look at that,' he proposed. 'That's a good idea,' Callender said. 'Why don't you go and put the kettle on?' The moment he'd gone, Callender said: 'Let's get out of here.'

'But what about the carpet?'

'Never mind the bloody carpet. Scram.'

Outside in Cornhill the rain had come on again and we took the bottles into an alleyway and had a look at them. They were all ruined, which meant a loss of fifteen bob each: all I'd earned in the past two days and half a crown besides. Callender said he'd had enough and was off to the bookie's to check on the first of his second favourites, but I figured I might as well go back to the office and get some more of the lotion. Fact is, I was down to my last five bob and I had a feeling that wouldn't be enough for an evening with Susie. When I got back to Doughty Street I found Hastings sitting in the main office, cutting his fingernails with a pair of scissors. 'You're early,' he said.

'Sold a couple of bottles,' I lied, handing him the fifteen bob. 'Thought I'd better stock up.' I could see Hastings had me marked down as a likely lad. This time he even gave me one of his Gold Flakes to smoke. Then he said:

'Literary bloke, aren't you?'

How he'd found that out I had no idea. 'In a

manner of speaking.'

'Thought so.' There was a pause, so I had time to wonder what was coming. Had Hastings written a novel he wanted me to read? Would he like me to introduce him to T.S. Eliot? You could never tell. In the end he said:

'What do you think of J.B. Priestley?'

Well, that was easy enough to answer. 'I liked *The Good Companions*,' I told him, 'but I thought *Angel Pavement* went on a bit.'

Hastings was about to light another Gold Flake from the end of the one he was smoking, and was busily tapping it on the polished surface of the desk. 'That's what my wife reckoned,' he said, interestedly.

Christ knew how long this might have gone on. As it was, one of the other chaps barged in with a leaking Ceps flask that he reckoned had given him psoriasis, so I left them to it and walked back to Threadneedle Street in the rain. It was after lunch now, and quiet, with nothing much doing, but in the end, after a Cep that lasted all of fifteen minutes, I managed to sell a bottle to an old girl in a dress shop. That meant another half-crown to spend on Susie. After that I just mooched about, walked back to the West End and had a coffee in a milk bar, checked myself in a mirror to see that I looked all right, and thought about things. Mostly I thought about Susie, but funnily enough I couldn't get the memory of Hastings out of my head. Who'd have thought he'd have been so keen on J.B. Priestley?

*   *   *

She was already standing at the bar of the

Wheatsheaf when I arrived, punctually at three minutes to eight, talking to an old letch named Shuttleworth, who I knew would be angling to cut me out if I didn't shift him. As it turned out, I needn't have worried because she came bouncing over to me, waving her hand like someone practising semaphore signals.

'I'm sorry I was early,' she said.

'I'm sorry I was late.'

'I expect you were writing something, weren't you?' she said.

'As a matter of fact, I was.'

'Gracious! Are you writing another story? Or a novel?'

'Neither,' I said. 'I was writing a poem.'

After that the conversation stopped for a moment and I took a good look at her, just to be sure everything was as I remembered. She had her hair twisted back with a couple of gypsy earrings on either side and one of those A-line skirts that were all the rage just then, and I suppose I must have made it a bit obvious because she smiled a touch awkwardly and said:

'You said if I came to the Wheatsheaf you'd show me some writers.'

Which was a bit of a fixer, because looking round the bar—it was early for Soho and only a few of the regulars were in—there wasn't a writer in sight. But I was determined to make the evening go with a swing, so I scooted over to the bar, well out of earshot, buttonholed a middle-aged dipsomaniac called Parkinson who owed me a favour, and said:

'How would you like to earn a drink?'

'Two would be nice,' Parkinson said, once he'd got over the surprise.

'Well, if I bring that young lady in the corner over here, just pretend you've written something, will you?'

'Written what?' As well as being a dipsomaniac, Parkinson was famously slow on the uptake.

'I don't f——g know. A Greek tragedy in five acts. Nature poetry. Anything.'

Queerly enough, old Parkinson did me proud. He had that characteristic, which occurs only in the most assiduous drunks, of believing in every word he said, and he spun Susie an incredible yarn about writing film scripts down at Teddington for the quota quickies and an epic poem about Florence Nightingale he was working on in his spare time. Susie, I could see, was drinking it all down, along with her gin and tonic. When Parkinson shuffled off to the gents and showed no sign of coming back— he was known to fall asleep in there with his head against the cistern and have to be routed out by the landlord—I steered her over to an unoccupied table by the door for a tête-à-tête.

'I don't even know your name.'

'It's Susie. Susie Chamberlain.'

She was twenty-three, it turned out, had done a couple of years training as a commercial artist and, what with the slump, was working as a secretary for a character called Rasmussen, halfway along the City Road.

'What's he do when he's at home?' I asked.

'It's difficult to say. Some of the time he sells diamonds. But he goes out rather a lot.'

'And what do you do?'

'Oh, there are letters to type. And I answer the phone when he's not there.'

'How often does he go out?'

'That would be telling.'

It sounded odd to me, but I couldn't have cared less. In fact Rasmussen could have been a lion-tamer, unless he'd wanted me to sit in the cage with him.

The pub was filling up now, and there were some real writers scrounging drinks at the bar, but I reckoned I'd done my duty. We were getting on like a house on fire and at least once she reached out and grabbed my hand as it lay on the table-top. And then, would you believe it, just as nine o'clock struck and I was wondering if the money would stretch to another couple of rounds, she looked at her watch and said:

'You're going to think me terribly rude, but I promised I'd be back at Kensal Green soon.'

'Why's that then?'

'It's my friend. I said I'd help her write a letter. She's having trouble with her young man.'

'Can't she write a letter to her young man on her own?'

'She says she won't know what to say.'

'Couldn't it wait until tomorrow?'

'Her young man's going to Leeds in the morning.'

She was halfway out of the pub now, with me following behind. Parkinson, who'd finally been prised out of the gents, was staring at me sardonically.

'Look,' she said, putting her head so close to mine I could smell the scent rising off her neck. 'You're awfully nice. Why don't you come and meet me from work tomorrow? Come about half-past five. Can you do that? I promise I'll be there.' Well, I'd heard worse ideas, so I waved her off

41

from the doorway, watching the A-line skirt until it disappeared round the corner of Rathbone Place. Twenty yards down the pavement she turned to look back at me and I flicked my finger up to my temple in a mock salute.

Once she'd gone I thought I might as well be getting back myself. Truth to tell, I was finding being back on the door-to-door hard work and all the afternoon I'd been yawning like a Burbank starlet the morning after the audition. Still, though, heading back on the bus to Paddington I had this queer feeling that the day wasn't quite over yet, not by a long chalk, and sure enough, after letting myself into the house with my latch key, I found the hall light on and a tall character in his forties I'd seen hanging around the place once or twice before smoking a fag halfway up the staircase.

'How do,' I said, making to move past him, but he wheeled round and stuck a fat hand out against the wall.

'Not so fast,' he said. 'You got any money?'

'That's between me and Mrs Fanshawe,' I said, indignant-like.

'Well, I'm her brother, and unless you can find that six quid you won't be skippering here tonight.'

For a moment I wondered about sloshing him, but he was a big bloke, two-stone heavier than me at least, and besides all my stuff was up there. 'Look,' I said, 'I'll be honest with you. I'm cleaned out, but I'll have money tomorrow. Can't it wait till then?'

'No it f——g can't. It's been waiting a month. Fair do's. Come back here tomorrow with the six quid and you get your room back. If not, door stays shut until you do.'

42

'Look here,' I said in my toniest voice, 'I think it would be better if I spoke to Mrs Fanshawe.'

'No can do,' he said. 'That's the trouble with my sister. She's got a heart of gold.' Fact is, he had me over a barrel and he knew it.

'Couldn't I get a few things to see me through until the morning?' I asked, but he just sniffed.

'Seen your sort before, chum. Three-to-one you'd be shinning down the pipe with a suitcase.'

Anyway, there I was out on the pavement at ten o'clock at night with nowhere to go. First things first, I thought, so I leaned on the front gate and had a cigarette, the last one in the packet, and counted out all the money I had in my pocket, just in case old Ma Fanshawe was looking up from her basement. There was fivepence-halfpenny, which was a bit of a facer, as the cheapest bed you could get in London in those days was sevenpence, and that meant going down to Lambeth and letting the bugs crawl over you in a sheet that hadn't seen soapsuds since Christmas. But I wasn't beat yet, I thought. The solution, as I saw it (and I'd been in fixes like this before) was to head back to the Wheatsheaf, where I was pretty well known— it didn't shut till eleven, which was a bonus—and see if I couldn't put together the price of a night's lodging.

After I'd worked out what to do I cheered up a bit, and even blue'd a penny out of the fivepence-halfpenny on another cigarette out of the machine round by the corner of Paddington station to smoke on the bus. There was no one much on it, just a very old conductor with white hair who was clearly feeling the strain as he kept parking himself on the seats between stops. The rain was drifting in against

43

the window, which made the streets beyond look kind of aquarium-like, as if the people were shoals of fish, and for some reason—probably the memory of Susie waving to me in Rathbone Place—I started thinking about all the women I'd known. It was quite a catalogue when you came to think of it: Mrs Bence-Jones back at the accountancy firm in Hove, and Dorothy who taught in the girl's school at Chichester, and Ethel who I'd even got as far as taking home to meet the old lady, not to mention Netta.

This set me thinking—not just about women, but the things they wanted. What did women want? It was a good question, and I'd never got to the bottom of it. Some of them wanted you to marry them and some of them didn't, and the ones who wanted you to were furious when you didn't ask them, while the ones who didn't were equally furious when you did. Did they want power? It depended on what you meant by power, I decided, as the bus chugged down Oxford Street under the flaring gaslights. At any rate Mrs Bence-Jones, who I could see, picture-framed in the doorway of the bed-sitting room with a pair of lorgnettes jammed on the bridge of her nose, made Genghis Khan look like an amateur. I had the sense to realize that none of this was doing me any good, so I reached into my jacket pocket where I sometimes kept notepaper for jotting down bits of overheard conversation, only to turn up a letter Netta had written to me. 'Dear James,' it went:

I am sure you will realize that after your exploits last night there is nothing more that we could possibly say to each other. It was a great pity that

44

you had to behave in the way that you did, as it made me understand that I was a fool to believe the things that you said to me. My mother asks me to tell you that she is prepared to overlook the business of the tablecloth. You may keep the Michael Arlen book, which I confess that I never liked. I must insist that you do not attempt to communicate with me again. I repeat, everything is over between us.
    Netta

The really ghastly thing was that I couldn't for the life of me remember what I was supposed to have done.

*   *   *

I don't mind telling you that finding that letter really stopped me in my tracks. All the way up Rathbone Place I was thinking about Netta and the times we'd had and wondering—that was the way my mind worked sometimes—why she hadn't liked the Michael Arlen book. But ten seconds in the Wheatsheaf was enough to drive her clean out of my head, for the simple reason that the place was practically empty, with just a couple of cab drivers drinking halves of stout and Muriel the barmaid drying glasses with a tea towel. 'Where's everyone gone?' I asked, and Muriel put down the pint pot she was drying and said: 'Didn't you know? Old Mr Sotherton died. They're having a wake down in Dean Street.' Now, I'd known old Sotherton he was a real Soho veteran, so old that he remembered meeting Thackeray or someone when he was a boy—and in normal circumstances

45

I'd have been down to Dean Street like a shot. But the twopencehalfpenny—I'd spent another twopence on the bus fare was burning a hole in my pocket. It was already a quarter to eleven, which meant everything would be shutting down soon, so I nipped out of the pub and went to a coffee place on the corner where I reckoned I'd be certain of meeting someone who'd lend me half a crown, which was enough to get you into a Rowton House or even a commercial hotel in those days. Queer thing was, the coffee place was deserted, too, and by eleven I was back in the Tottenham Court Road with the people flowing past in streams, wondering just exactly what I was going to do with myself.

It was a warmish night, and I knew if the worst came to the worst there was always the Embankment or one of the garden squares in Pimlico—you bunked over the railings and tried to get out before the gardener arrived in the morning. But I've got my pride about where I lay my head and I'd never yet been reduced to the Embankment or Eccleston Square. In the end, I went up to a copper on points duty and asked him what he would advise? 'Waiting room at King's Cross station,' he said straight off. 'They have to keep it open for the overnight trains and the attendant clocks off at midnight.' By this stage I was dog tired and by rights I should have taken a bus up to King's Cross, but I didn't want to break into the twopence-halfpenny. The streets were thinning out now and the pubs in Goodge Street were disgorging their customers. I limped along the Tottenham Court Road thinking that if I couldn't sort myself out in the next couple of days it would have to be goodbye to London and maybe a spell with the old lady again—that was how bad it was.

Anyhow, coming into King's Cross I fell in with a little chap carrying a Gladstone bag under one arm. 'You look as if you're heading the same way as me, young man,' he said.

'Waiting room,' I told him.

'That's the ticket. Trick is to cover yourself in advance.' He explained: 'If they think you're just there to have a kip, attendant'll chuck you out before he goes off duty.' We were getting near to the door of the waiting room now, where a big chap in a uniform and a peaked cap stood staring. 'Here we are,' he said in an artificially loud voice, holding the door open. 'Aberdeen sleeper leaves at half-past twelve, so we'll just sit down here for a mo.'

'Thanks for the tip,' I said, as we lowered ourselves into our seats. There was no one much about and the attendant, having given us the once-over, had drifted off somewhere else. 'You come here often then?'

'Now and again. I do it to get away from the wife.' I'd begun to look at the posters advertising seaside holidays, with one about Skegness being so bracing, but the mention of his wife drew me back. 'You married?' he asked.

'Never met the right girl.'

'Well, you're well out of that,' he said, hardly listening. 'If I didn't come here a couple of nights a month I'd strangle the old bitch, straight up I would.'

'Would you really?' I asked, interested. 'What's so bad about her?'

'That depends,' he said. 'It depends on which way you look at it.'

47

After that he went quiet for a bit and I watched the clock on the wall tick round to just before midnight.

The two or three genuine-looking passengers had gone by now, hauling their suitcases with them over the carpet, and the place was starting to fill up with frayed types in mackintoshes and exiguous shoe leather. 'What happens now?' I asked.

'Nothing. You can go to sleep if you like, but you mustn't snore and you mustn't lie on the floor. Do that and the copper can have you up. Otherwise you can stay here till five, which is when the cafe over the way opens. Got any money?' I explained about the twopence-halfpenny. 'Well, if I were you I'd stick that in your shoes. There's some light-fingered b——ds in here sometimes. Here, you want to see what I've got in my case?'

'I don't mind.'

'All right,' he said, 'you take a look then.' God knew what it was going to be—for a half a minute I wondered if he had something nasty in there, like a severed head—but in the end he pulled out a row of war medals. 'See that?' he said. 'That's a Mons Star, that is. You don't see many of them around. They didn't give too many of them away.'

'You must be a very brave man.'

'Oh they're not mine,' he told me. 'I bought them in a shop. It's one of the things I argue about with my missus. She never liked it that I didn't fight in the war.'

A bit later I fell asleep for a while. It was a queer feeling, because however deeply asleep you thought you were you could always hear the coughs and snores of the people around you and feel the light boring into your eyes. Once I woke up and

48

found the little bloke with the case had moved off half-a-dozen seats away. Then when I came to again it was ten past three and he'd fallen asleep with his head practically across my shoulder and his mouth wide open. Gold fillings he had, which just goes to show. A copper put his head through the door, looked at one of the snorers, poked him in the chest with a finger as big as a frankfurter and went away again. For some reason I couldn't get back to sleep, so I picked up a copy of *Sketch* that someone had left on the floor. I read about Mrs Antrobus's party and Rolls Royces in Belgrave Square and what Mr Harry Melville, whoever he was, had said about it and the dainty little black dress worn by the Hon. Mrs Evelyn Henderson or someone, until all this merged into a dream about Susie taking off her black jumper, so that her essentials spilled out into my hands, and then suddenly it was gone five—grey and ghostly despite the light—and the little bloke was nudging me awake. 'Ho,' he said. 'You was far gone there. Yus indeed. All kinds of things you was saying to yourself. Come on. Cafe's open. Why don't we have a cup of tea? My treat.'

He was a decent old boy and pretty soon we were in the station cafe with half-a-dozen other of the blokes who'd been in the waiting room—you never saw so many unshaven faces!—drinking tea and eating penny buns, which was about all they had at that hour. When we'd finished, the little chap tapped his Gladstone bag and said: 'Well, I'd better be getting back to Borehamwood. What about you?' I explained about the carpet lotion and he said it didn't sound much of a job. 'It's not,' I said.

'Would a bob help?'

'Thanks but no thanks,' I said. 'You've stood me

a tea already.'

So I watched him walk off towards the tube and wondered what I was going to do with myself. It was still only about six o'clock and the offices didn't open until nine. Besides, apart from the penny bun I'd had nothing to eat since yesterday lunchtime and I knew I could do with a square meal. There was something I needed more than that, though, and in the end I went into a tobacconist's and spent twopence on a packet of five Park Drive. The tarts were coming off the night shift and piling into the street cafes. I stood and watched their white faces, like lard against the grey of the dawn, and listened to the click-clack of their high heels on the pavement.

Then it occurred to me that I ought to clean myself up a bit, so I nipped back into the gents at the station for a wash and brush-up. It was full of blokes like me, with bags under their eyes and fearful complexions, shaving with blunt razor-blades and bits of soap and ignoring the signs that said: THESE PREMISES ARE TO BE USED FOR CASUAL ABLUTIONS ONLY. When I'd finished washing I took a look in the mirror and, sure enough, I looked terrible. Curiously, though, I'd cheered up again. In fact, I even had a plan, which was to head for the City Road and see if I could find Susie's office. She mightn't be very pleased to see me, but I figured I could bum a bob or two for breakfast, put in a good day's work—as far away from Callender as possible—and then see if I could come to some kind of arrangement with Ma Fanshawe. So I headed off east through the City, with my halfpenny in one hand and a cigarette in the other, taking my time and seeing what there was to see. You get an odd crowd at seven o'clock in the morning: young sprigs in evening dress with wilted carnations in their buttonholes, swaying back to the tube after a night on the tiles; mysterious old women toting cardboard boxes God knows where; pale-faced girls who don't look like tarts but have clearly been up to something that daddy would despair of if he only knew. It takes all sorts, I suppose.

By half-past eight I was sitting by some railings next to Bunhill Fields. The grass had grown six feet high and there were tramps brewing tea in the shadow of the gravestones. Keeping an eye on what I'd worked out must be Susie's basement, I suddenly caught sight of the A-line skirt as she damned near walked into me. 'Susie,' I said, not wanting to startle her.

'What are you doing here?' she said. When I explained about being kicked out of my digs and the night at King's Cross she went all wide-eyed and concerned. You could tell that she thought it was the sort of thing writers did: feckless but kind of romantic at the same time. I'd clearly gone up 100 per cent in her estimation. 'Gracious,' she said. 'You must be starving.'

'I was wondering . . . Susie, you couldn't stand me a couple of bob, could you? I'll pay you back after I've been out on the round.'

'Don't be silly,' she said. 'As if I'd want paying back. Look, come into the office. Mr Rasmussen never gets in until half-past nine.'

'You're an angel.'

It turned out that her office was exactly where I'd thought it was: down some steps beneath a lopsided building that housed a disposable-razor concern, a tailor's and a black-lead company.

It was a queer kind of basement, with dust everywhere and lots of metal filing cabinets and bits of jewellery lying about, but I wasn't complaining, and while Susie took off her hat and coat—she was wearing another jumper even tighter than the last—I stared at a battered old roll-top desk where someone had left a sheet of cartridge paper with a rather good drawing of a street frontage with the distance between the shop-fronts picked out in blue ink. 'That's Mr Rasmussen's desk,' she said, by way of explanation. She rummaged in a drawer and pulled out a black cash-box. Inside there was a ten-bob note and a heap of silver. A bit shyly, she gave me the ten-bob note. 'I'll put it down as a sub in the petty cash,' she said. 'I often get a bit short myself by the end of the week.' After that we went back up to the street and had a cigarette each. They were the last two from the packet I'd bought at six o'clock that morning, which seemed a lifetime away.

It was a beautiful late-summer morning, and what with the ten bob and Susie and the smoke crackling in my lungs, I wasn't feeling too bad. 'Look, that's my boss coming,' Susie said, gesturing down the street. 'You'd better go now. He'll think I've been up to no good.'

'Well, you have, haven't you,' I said, 'in a manner of speaking,' and she laughed in a way that would have had Kublai Khan turning out the spare bedroom. I took a look along the pavement and there, forty yards away, was a spare-looking middle-aged bloke with a walrus moustache and a rolled umbrella over his arm. And then all of a sudden two things struck me. One was that I'd

52

seen this Rasmussen character somewhere before. Couldn't say where, but there was something about the set of his face that pulled me up. The other was that the drawing on the desk looked uncommonly like the outside of that place in Cornhill that Callender and I had been into the other day. But then Susie kissed me on the cheek and, of course, I forgot all about it.

SATURDAY AFTERNOON

*Nothing, it may be said, offers a more painful
contrast to the reflective voyager than the
City out of hours. For five and a half days in
the week the pavements around Cornhill are
all bustle, industry and communal purpose.
Here strides the financier, the bill-broker, the
stock-jobber, each bent sedulously upon his
daily task. Here, too, come the clerk, the typist
and the office lad, each in however modest a
way caught up in the romance of the ancient
streets through which they wander. But venture
east of the Strand after lunch time on Saturday
or late on a Sabbath morning and all you will
see are cats and caretakers, and Cornhill, that
bright indisputable tributary to the river of our
commercial life, is the most melancholy place on
earth.*

H.V. Morton, City Haunts and Homes *(1931)*

Mr Rasmussen sat in his basement office in the
City Road, beneath a winnowing fan that required
most of the documents on his desk to be secured by
paper clips and the morning newspaper that lay at
his elbow to be pinioned by a telephone directory.
It was half-past twelve on a Saturday afternoon
and the City was closing down for the weekend.
Mr Rasmussen's secretary, a vision of red hair and
white silk stockings, stood in the murky vestibule

fastening the metal clips of her coat with brisk little snaps. Above her head, where the window let out into the street, a procession of legs, weirdly truncated at the knee, could be seen heading north in the direction of Old Street station. Mr Rasmussen heard the sharp little detonations of the clips and saw the truncated legs, but paid them no attention. Unlike the stockbrokers' clerks heading to Old Street, he did not have a wife and children to go home to, and his time was his own.

'I'll be off then,' said the secretary, Miss Chamberlain, more red haired and silk-stockinged than ever in the half-light of the vestibule, and Mr Rasmussen, looking up from his desk as if the whole extraneous world bored him, only there to distract him from the real business of his life, said: 'Yes, that's right. You be off then.' He was a tall, thinnish, sandy-haired man, who looked forty in a good light and fifty in a bad one, but who now, in the gloom of the City Road, swam agelessly in its shadows, dressed in a grey suit and what might, depending on the exact width of its stripes, have been an I Zingari tie.

'I made that call to Scrimgeours,' Miss Chamberlain said, in a faintly challenging way, 'but they said it would have to stand over until Monday morning.'

Mr Rasmussen made a faint gesture with his hand, as if to imply that all manner of things would have to stand over until Monday morning, allowing Miss Chamberlain to escape out into the street, where a few minutes later her figure could be seen flying along the City Road, leaving the basement to her employer, the winnowing fan and the paper-strewn desk. When she had gone, Mr

55

Rasmussen approached the telephone on his desk, looked out a detail or two from a black notebook plucked from the inside pocket of his grey suit, and had the operator put him through to a number in Kensington, but there was no answer and after a moment or two he gave up the game as lost. There was a brisk movement overhead, suggesting bolts turning sharply in a door, which Mr Rasmussen imagined to be the sound of the people who owned the disposable-razor company on the ground floor shutting up shop. He listened carefully to the various subsidiary noises that followed in its wake. Finally, the clatter of feet passed away, a telephone that had been ringing in one of the upstairs offices was suddenly extinguished and the building fell into silence.

A casual observer descending from the street— one of the travelling salesmen, perhaps, in morning suits and spats come to sell carbon paper and typewriting supplies—who looked around Mr Rasmussen's basement, might have wondered from exactly what trade he took his income, or from what source derived the three pounds three shillings per week that Miss Chamberlain bore away to her bed-sitting room in Kensal Green each Saturday lunchtime. There were a few fragments of jewellery lying around the place, and half a necklace in a little glass jar on a table by the desk, along with various stockbrokers' directories and a financial manual or two, and a couple of squat packing cases jammed on top of each other by the door, but apart from this no clue as to what ravens fed him or how Messrs Chesterton & Co, the letting agents, whose plaque was on the outer door, extracted their rent. But whatever it was that he did, it was clear that Mr

Rasmussen took a positive pleasure in it.

Left alone in his vault, the procession of truncated legs replaced now by thin streaks of rain that smeared the glass, he luxuriated in his solitude, and did three or four little things that he would probably not have done had Miss Chamberlain's eye been upon him: he took a dirty kettle out of a recess near the packing cases and boiled himself a cup of tea, lit a Russian cigarette and blew out the smoke in a cloud above his head, and moved one or two of the ornaments on his desk decisively back and forth. There were some banknotes on the desk, held down by a rubber-stamping device, which he picked up, flicked through with his fingers and placed inside a gunmetal cash-box, and another newspaper, hidden beneath the first, which he browsed through very solemnly, taking no account of the business or political columns, but spending several moments over its society gossip.

It was by now about five minutes to two, and Mr Rasmussen, having drunk his tea, smoked his cigarette and secured his banknotes, stirred suddenly, as if all the previous activities were the merest whimsy. He put on his overcoat, planted a trilby hat on his head, double-locked the door of his office and climbed the dozen steps that led to the street. Here, as he had foreseen, the pavements were deserted—the clerks and the typewriting girls and the smart young men from the insurance offices had all gone away home—and he found that he could walk southwards past the western edge of Finsbury Square and Finsbury Pavement without hindrance. Again, anyone who passed him in the street might have noticed that he carried under his arm a sheaf of commercial agents' particulars and that these embarrassed or irritated him in some way, as he was forever rolling them up into a cylinder or attempting to stow them in the pocket of his coat. Reaching the point at which Moorgate meets London Wall, he turned abruptly east and walked for perhaps ten minutes through a maze of small streets behind the Bank of England before emerging with a certain fixity of purpose into the region of Cornhill.

On the further side of Cornhill, at the point where it joins Leadenhall Street, there was a Lyons tea shop, very quiet now in the wake of the Saturday lull, but evidently just the kind of place that Mr Rasmussen found congenial, for a further few minutes saw him seated in its front window, a second cup of tea at his elbow, surveying the frontages of the shops on the opposite side with a keen interest. There was not, as it happened, a great deal to see. Directly opposite Mr Rasmussen's window was a tailor's shop in which fanciful representations of the Prince of Wales and the Duke of York could be seen bowing to one another against a frieze of cheap collars and wash-leather gloves. Beyond this was the premises of the East and City laundry, the window quite clouded over with steam and a delivery van packed with brown-paper parcels by the door. Further still was a jeweller's plate glass displaying the name of Cornhill Chambers, and beyond that a tobacconist's shop with a Grenadier guard towering by its entrance. All this was at ground level, but Mr Rasmussen, lingering over his tea, barely examined it. His gaze was fixed just above the shop-fronts, where an agent's board advertised offices to let, and some very dirty windows suggested that the letting

58

was not proving particularly easy to accomplish.

He sat there for a full ten minutes, the tea growing cold before him, staring at this unpromising vista, and then, suddenly, got up from his table, paid his bill and strolled out into the street. He wandered desultorily along on the opposite side, poked his head in at the door of the fifty-shilling tailor, looked at the Grenadier and the half-dozen dusty packets of cigarettes over which this custodian stood guard, moved back past the jeweller's plate glass and stopped a yard or two before the hot and steamy exterior of the laundry. The TO LET sign, he now calculated, but without raising his eyes to do so, was directly above his head. The entrance hall of the laundry, he noted at the same time, was set to one side of a wider street door, the other side of which a flight of stairs wound away in the direction of an upper floor. It was by now about half-past two, very grey with more rain sweeping in from the west, and Mr Rasmussen, keeping one eye on the laundry door, darted swiftly to his left and made his way up the staircase. He did this not quite silently, but not perhaps with the air of a man who wants attention drawn to his movements. At the top of the stairs was a glass-panelled door with a further TO LET sign hung over its lower panel. Mr Rasmussen reached into the inside pocket of his coat and brought out what looked like a metal pencil, inserted it into the lock, gave a couple of twists and admitted himself into the premises.

Once inside, and having shut the door behind him, he stopped to take his bearings in the half-light. As he had suspected, he stood in the vestibule of a suite of rooms running off to the left—that is, above the jeweller's shop rather than the laundry, the murmur of whose machinery he could still hear faintly in the distance beneath him. There was a movement in the debris at his feet, and a mouse ran off into the wainscoting—he could see its beady eyes staring up from the murk—and he staggered a little on his feet and wished that he had brought a torch. By degrees he accustomed his vision to the gloom and began to wander along the corridor that led away to his left, peering through the half-open doors and casting his eye over the abandoned lumber. In one of the rooms he found a set of dusty scales and some wicker baskets—altogether ghostly in the gathered-up shadow—and this suggested to him that the firm who had previously rented the premises dealt in tea.

He knew something of tea and, obeying some queer impulse he could not quite fathom, he bent his head over one of the wicker baskets and inhaled the faintest scent of jasmine. Something of the strangeness of his errand occurred to him and he straightened his back, thinking how odd it was that he should be sifting through the paraphernalia of a defunct tea-broker in Cornhill as the rain beat upon the window and the mice scurried across the drugget at his feet. He moved on into another room where there was a map on the wall of the Indian shipping routes and a copy of *Kelly's Directory* of the City of London for 1923. A fragment of cracked mirror hung next to the map and his face caught in it as he turned away, changed beyond all recognition.

Mr Rasmussen laughed and continued his exploration, turning into a third room that contained only an ancient jellygraph machine and a pile of rags, and laughed again but, it might have been suspected, without finding the thing he was looking for. There were some newspapers on the floor, and he picked up one of them to find a lively account of the difficulties faced by Mr Snowden in compiling his first budget. Finally—it was very dark now and the light from the street window behind him had all but given out—he came to a last room, built on a slightly larger scale than the rest. It was quite empty, apart from a pair of rusty-iron chair mouldings and a faded portrait of Queen Mary in her coronation robes, but seeing it, and calculating its distance from the staircase, Mr Rasmussen's whole demeanour seemed to change. He began by walking the perimeter of the room—the dust sprang up and befouled his shoes—estimating its extent and on one occasion pulling up the edge of the grey carpet to inspect the parquet that lay beneath. Then, returning to his original vantage point, he strode quickly into the centre of the room, lifted his left foot and stamped twice. There was another cascade of dust, and a faint, hollow reverberation. This suggested to Mr Rasmussen that the room beneath was at least as wide as the one in which he now stood, and that it was not reinforced by any stronger material than the parquet and the plaster beneath it.

It was now so dark that he struck a match from a packet of Swan Vestas fished out of his pocket and held it out at arm's length while he inspected a list of old commodity prices that were displayed on the wall ahead. The sound of a clock striking three suggested to Mr Rasmussen that he had spent long enough on this investigation and, wrapping his coat around him, and making sure to close any door that had been opened during the course of his visit, he made his way back to the outer door, refastened it and stood outside on the tiny landing, collecting his thoughts. It seemed to him as he stood there that he detected some slight change in the atmosphere, something to do with the absence of light and noise. After a second or two he established both that the laundry had ceased its operations for the day and that the street door was locked. What should Mr Rasmussen do with himself? The metal cylinder would have the street door open in a moment, but he reminded himself that he had no way of knowing who might be on the other side when he opened it. Therefore, moving softly down the staircase, he turned carefully into the doorway of the laundry company. This door had only a single, inferior lock and, having forced it, he moved silently through the laundry—very quiet and ghastly now, with immense sheets dripping from the cross-wires and the air still full of moisture—until he found a small room in the back part of the premises with a couple of windows and the promise of an alleyway behind it.

Again, the fastenings were no match for Mr Rasmussen. Five minutes later he was dusting down his trousers in a culvert, which as he had predicted, brought him back onto the northern side of Cornhill, a stone's throw from the Lyons tea shop where he had begun his journey. A glance at his watch showed that it was a quarter past three. Shoulders hunched into his overcoat and a queer look of satisfaction on his face, he began to walk westward in the direction of Fleet Street, a small, purposeful speck slowly engulfed in the shadow of the descending day.

6

UNFINISHED BUSINESS

Sound Advice for the Salesman:
III. Resourcefulness

Remember! No two sales are alike. For every customer who greets you with open arms and a ready smile, there will be another who is resistant to even the most amusing 'patter'. The successful salesman is not an automaton with a dreary catalogue of tried and tested phrases. No, he is a live-wire who judges each commercial opportunity on its merits and responds to it in kind. Does the customer, for example, take a pride in his garden? If so, a few horticultural remarks will invariably ensure a sympathetic hearing. Does the woman of the house seem especially well-dressed? Then venture a discreetly favourable comment on her apparel. It is always said of the best salesman that he can sell a pair of spectacles to a blind man. Salesmen—make this your motto!

Abraxas Salesman's Handbook

'Thirty-seven and six,' Hastings said, writing down the figures in the little black notebook he had on his desk.

'Not bad. D'you want the commission now, or wait till the end of the week?'

'End of the week'll do fine.'

'Suit yourself.' Hastings reached into the packet of Gold Flake next to the notebook and lit a fag off the stub of the one he was finishing. 'There's some chaps want paying for every sale they make. Come back here for the commission a half-crown at a time. Can't think why.'

Well, I could have told him.

It was three weeks now since I'd been turned out of my digs that night and I'd been keeping my head down. As I'd reckoned, the digs question had sorted itself out. I'd crept back to Ma Fanshawe's the next afternoon, figuring the brother wouldn't be around just then—he wasn't—offered ten bob down and a promise to pay off the balance at ten bob a week and even got an apology into the bargain. Plus the *London Mercury*, one of the posh literary papers, had taken that poem I'd been writing. What they paid wouldn't keep Ma Fanshawe in hairgrips for a week, but it bucked me no end to think of sharing space with Walter de la Mare and John Drinkwater. Why, even the old lady had heard of them. The only fly in the ointment, curiously enough, was Susie. I'd seen her a couple of times, once in the Wheatsheaf again, another time in a Lyons over the road from where she worked, but she hadn't stayed long and there was more talk about the friend who needed help writing letters to her young man (he was in Leeds now, playing fast and loose with a girl who worked in a dry-cleaning shop, lucky b——r.) Anyway, what with needing to earn more money to pay off Ma Fanshawe, and thinking about the poem and how it would look in the *Mercury*, I wasn't too fussed about this. I knew things would work themselves out one way or another: they always do.

'Tell you what,' Hastings said, all matey-like. 'Seeing how well you're doing, you can go back on the City round with Callender if you fancy. He was asking after you just the other day.'

Another thing that had occupied me in the last three weeks was staying clear of Callender. I'd had enough of his fiddles, and of standing outside bookies' offices while he went to collect his winnings. Come to think of it, I hadn't seen him for a fortnight.

'Actually, I'm fine in Bayswater,' I said.

'Suit yourself,' Hastings said, lighting his third cigarette. He really did live off fags: a kind of hungry gleam came into his eyes when he put one in his mouth. He dropped his voice a tone and leaned confidentially over the desk. 'He's a funny bloke, that Callender.'

This wasn't exactly news to me, but I played dumb. 'How so?'

'Was a bloke in here asking for him yesterday. Little chap with a toothbrush moustache waxed up at the ends. Put the fear of God into me when I saw him. Thought it was someone from the tax office. But it was Callender he wanted, not me.'

'Policeman?'

'Didn't say. None of my business, of course.'

I liked Hastings, who was always good for a fag these days and had even stood me a pint the other Friday lunchtime. Roper hadn't been seen for a week. It was rumoured that he had DTs. As I was hauling my canvas bag off the chair, Hastings said:

'Hang on a mo. There was something I meant to ask you.'

'Fire away.'

'What do you think of Warwick Deeping?'

Well, I'd read *Sorrel and Son*, like everybody else. 'A bit middlebrow for my taste,' I said.

*   *   *

On the bus heading west along Oxford Street I reflected that I was getting the hang of this salesman's lark. The trick, as I saw it, was to remember that there was only one group of people who were ever going to buy anything, and that was old ladies. Anyone else—housewives, blokes, parlour-maids—was a waste of time. The other trick, I'd learned, was to take things gradually. Whether or not they were desperate for a chat, the old ladies didn't like to be hurried. At the moment I had half-a-dozen of them on the go who hadn't bought anything yet but were just on the point of taking the plunge. You had to take it slow.

It was getting towards September now and the weather'd changed. Pale sky up above the heights beyond Hampstead. Fine rain coming down across the grey streets. All this upset me a bit. It made me think of other autumns, back steaming open the mail in the hut at Southern Coastal Command, drinking mulled ale in those Sussex pubs with Netta, or loafing in Mrs Bence-Jones's bed-sitting room watching her wind the grandfather clock. Lugging my kit off the bus I suddenly felt moth-eaten and ground-down in a way I hadn't for ages, depressed about Susie, and thinking that I'd never make anything of myself, that I ought to square things with the old lady. After a cig and a sale at one of those big houses in Inverness Terrace, I bucked up a bit and decided I'd go and see Mrs Grayson.

Mrs Grayson was one of my old ladies, and this must have been the fourth or fifth time I'd called on her. She lived in one of those little semis in the side-streets off Queensway, which looked as if it had last seen a decorator about the time of the Diamond Jubilee—Mr Grayson had died in 1903, apparently—but she was a nice old girl. Plus, the place was full of huge, shabby carpets that clearly needed all the attention I could give them.

'Why, it's Mr Ross,' said Mrs Grayson when she opened the door. 'I had a feeling I might see you this morning.'

She was a wispy little grey-haired number who couldn't have been far short of eighty, and she liked what I call respectful heartiness.

'Well, Mrs Grayson,' I said loudly. 'It must be a week since I last called by. As you know, I never neglect a potential customer. I hope I find you well this morning?'

'Oh, I don't know. Nothing special. I have a cough, you know, that simply never goes away.'

Mrs Grayson's cough. I'd learned all about that. How it kept her awake at nights. How the doctor couldn't shift it. How she'd tried cocktails of patent medicine on it, all to no avail. But I tried to look sympathetic, while at the same time unloading the Ceps kit just to let her know that it wasn't a social call.

'I expect you'd like a cup of tea, Mr Ross?'

'That would be very nice, Mrs Grayson.'

While she was off in the kitchen—I could hear the cough rumbling away like distant gunfire—I took another squint round the drawing room, which never failed to fascinate me. God knows, the old lady had some junk in her house, but Mrs

67

Grayson outdid her on every count. There was a picture of her husband in bicycling gear—pepper-and-salt knickerbockers and a nankeen jacket—that must have been taken in 1880, and a monstrous aspidistra quite seven feet tall growing in a kind of barrel.

'Now,' said Mrs Grayson, reappearing with the tea on a tray—it was always very good tea, the best I'd had on the door-to-doors—'I expect you're going to try and sell me something, aren't you?'

'You anticipate my thoughts, Mrs Grayson,' I said. 'But I can assure you, speaking objectively, that your carpets would benefit from the service we have to offer. Why, it wouldn't surprise me if there were 3lbs or more of dirt concealed in this very carpet we're standing on at the moment.'

'Dear me, that does sound a lot.'

'And this increases the chance—not wishing to alarm you, Mrs Grayson—of the material rotting before your eyes.'

'Well, I don't want that. Just think if one had people round and the carpets began to rot. I think perhaps I had better buy two of your bottles.'

'A wise decision, Mrs Grayson,' I boomed. 'I should perhaps point out that your house, from what I've seen of it, contains a very large amount of carpeting. Why, I'd estimate it at nearly a quarter of an acre.'

'Three bottles then.'

There was another fusillade of coughing as she went off to get her purse. Meanwhile, I congratulated myself on a job well done: another seven-and-six for Ma Fanshawe and, if I played my cards right, I'd get a repeat order.

When Mrs Grayson came back she had a puzzled

expression on her face. 'Dear me. I could have sworn I had a pound note in my purse. I must have given it to the gentleman who called about the whist-club subscription.'

I was feeling all open-hearted after making the sale, so I said: 'Never mind, Mrs Grayson, you keep the bottles and I'll come back tomorrow for the money.' And have another pot of your Pekoe Points, I nearly added.

'Oh no. I don't think that would be right. I think the best thing would be if I were to write you an IOU.'

And so she produced a piece of notepaper and wrote on it, in an immensely florid and antique hand, that Oenone Grayson promised to pay Mr James Ross of the Abraxas Carpet Cleaning Company the sum of twenty-two shillings and sixpence at any time convenient to him. You couldn't say fairer than that, I thought, and standing on the doorstep I went so far as to shake the old girl's hand.

'I shall have the pleasure of seeing you again tomorrow, Mrs Grayson.'

'You certainly shall, Mr Ross.'

Queer! It was then on the doorstep, just as I was backing away into the street with the kit-bag banging against my heels, that I had my blinding moment of revelation. Now I knew where I'd seen Susie's boss, Mr Rasmussen, before. It had been in that old copy of *Police News*.

*   *   *

When I got back from work later that afternoon—I'd sold another three bottles along the way, which wasn't too bad—I rooted out the copy of *Police News* from down the side of the armchair and took another look. It was Rasmussen all right, called something else of course—McTavish or Montmorency—but indisputably the same man. The letterpress hadn't much to say about what he'd actually done, but you got the impression that all information would be warmly welcomed. After I'd made this discovery I lay on the bed in my shirt and trousers and smoked a cigarette, wondering what, if anything, I ought to do. What was Susie doing working for someone who got his mug printed in *Police News*? Did she know he was a crook? Was she his accomplice, even? Outside, the rain had stopped and it turned all kind of Indian-summery with light spilling in through the window and making the room look a whole lot more dusty than it really was; I wished I'd got something to do that night instead of sitting there trying to write one of my stories. It's a grand old life, literature, but you need to get out now and again, you know. In the end I got out my gold-nibbed pen and the box of Basildon Bond stationery Netta had given me and wrote some letters.

Darling Mums,
Sorry I haven't been in touch for so long, but work has been simply fearful. Did I tell you I gave up the marine underwriting and am working on the Londoner's Diary *on the* Standard? *They are rather vulgar people, but quite amusing. Also, I seem to have been taken up by the smart young set—Evelyn Henderson and her husband and the Pellys and the people who meet at Mrs Antrobus's—so it is all*

70

rather exhausting. If you could see your way to advancing me ten guineas for a new evening suit, I should be awfully obliged.
Goodbye for now,
James

The stuff about the young smart set, which I'd got from the *Sketch*, I knew the old lady would lap up. The second letter, which was addressed to the chief superintendent at West End Central, took a bit more time.

Dear Sir,
You may be interested to know that the man named McTavish whose picture appeared in Police News *recently is actually called Rasmussen. He has an office in the City Road, between Bunhill Fields and Old Street station. Trusting that this information will be of use to you.*
'A well-wisher.'

As well as not signing my name, I left off the address, too. I wanted all this to be strictly incognito, you see. When I got back from posting the letters in the box at the corner of the street, I had my second shock of the day. There, standing outside the door of my room, was Susie. I couldn't think of anything to say, so I just gaped.

'I got given the afternoon off,' she said. 'I just happened to be passing and I thought I'd drop by. You don't mind, do you?'

No prizes for guessing what the answer to that was. She was looking gorgeous, too, in one of those summery frocks and a jacket with little tassels that she smoothed down nervously with her hands.

'How did you get in?' I asked. Ma Fanshawe was chary of 'callers', and put female ones in the same category as plague rats.

'Oh, the front door was open and I just walked up. You don't mind, do you?' she asked again. 'Only I've always wanted to see where you lived.'

'Of course I don't. You'd better come in.' I was wondering if there was anything incriminating on display, but she didn't seem to care. She went straight for the bookcase and stood there looking at it with a kind of glow in her eyes.

'If I'd have known you were coming,' I said, 'I'd have tidied up a bit.'

'I think it's a lovely room. Just where I'd imagined a writer would live.'

'How's your friend?' I asked. 'The one who was having trouble with her young man.'

'She's very upset. She went all the way to Leeds the other day on the train to meet him, and then she saw him coming out of a shop with another girl.'

'That's bad.'

'He's Jewish, you see, and I said: "What can you expect?"'

'Shall I make you a cup of tea?' I asked.

'That would be very nice.'

'I'm afraid there's only the one chair.'

'That's all right. I'll sit on the floor. I don't mind. We can be bohemian. Like the people in Chelsea.'

Well, I didn't mind either. Then what I'd been thinking about before she arrived came back to me, and I said: 'How's your Mr Rasmussen?'

'Actually he hasn't been about much recently. He's opening a new office. I mean, as well as our one. Somewhere in Bloomsbury.'

72

'What's he going to do there?'

'I don't know. Sell gramophones or something.' She put down her tea cup. 'You're awfully nice,' she said.

The next thing I knew I was down on the carpet—which could have done with some of the Abraxas cleaning lotion—kissing her for all I was worth. She let me do this for a moment or so and then pulled away.

'I hope you don't think I spend my time visiting men in their rooms?'

'I'm sure you don't.'

'You're awfully nice . . . Here . . .'

A couple more moments went by. She smelled of, I don't know, not new-mown hay or the things girls are supposed to smell of, but parma violets. The room was full of sunshine from the window and the dust-motes danced in the light. As always on these occasions I had the feeling that I wanted things to go on like this forever. Then, all of a sudden, there was a terrific double knock on the door—mercifully I'd taken the precaution of turning the key beforehand—and a rattle on the door handle that was fit to wake the dead.

'Christ!' I said.

'Who is it?' she asked, not seeming especially put out.

'Mrs Fanshawe. My landlady. One moment Mrs Fanshawe,' I yelled out. 'I'll just open the door.'

Fortunately Susie was a quick worker. By the time I'd buttoned my shirt and was unfastening the door, she was parked soberly in the armchair with the empty tea cup in her lap, looking as if butter wouldn't melt in her mouth—which was more than could be said for me.

I don't think I've told you about Mrs Fanshawe. She would have been about forty-five to fifty, tending to stoutness, with hair that was ash-blonde four-fifths of the time and a kind of salmon pink in the week after she'd had it marcelled at Madame Selina's in the High Street. You didn't give her any cheek, either.

'This is Miss Chamberlain,' I said. 'My landlady, Mrs Fanshawe. We were just having tea.'

'Pleased to meet you, I'm sure,' said Mrs Fanshawe a bit coolly.

There wasn't exactly a rule about not having women in your room but I could see that I'd blotted my copybook more effectively than if I'd let the rent run over for a year. I hadn't bargained for Susie, though, who put down her tea cup and rose out of the chair.

'I'm delighted to meet you, Mrs Fanshawe. I've heard so much about you from James—Mr Ross. He always tells me how well looked after he is here.'

'Does he now?' Mrs Fanshawe said.

'Yes. He's always talking about how kind you are to him.'

'Really?' replied Mrs Fanshawe.

Christ, I thought to myself, they'll be making up a bridge four together at this rate. 'Is there anything I can do for you, Mrs Fanshawe?' I enquired politely.

It was the feeblest stuff about the downstairs hall being redecorated next week and a hope that the smell of the paint wouldn't be too inconvenient—it was three-to-one the old girl had been listening at the keyhole for the last ten minutes—but I thanked her and she shuffled back down the stairs with the

74

air, I thought, of a cat who's seen a mouse whisked out of its jaws at the very last moment by an unseen hand.

'Christ!' I said again, when she'd gone.

'She seems very nice,' said Susie guilelessly. 'Not at all what I'd expected.'

If I'd any hopes of another session down on the carpet, they were quickly extinguished.

'I think I'd better be going,' she said.

'Do you have to?'

'Yes I must. Really.'

'When can I see you again?'

'Soon.'

'You've forgotten this.'

'So I have . . . I'll put it on when I get back.'

'Goodbye then.'

'Goodbye . . . darling.'

And then she was gone, back down the creaking staircase, and I lay on the bed and smoked a cigarette, and thought that the people who write about this kind of thing in books always get it wrong, because it isn't funny at all.

*   *   *

What with working so hard and the business with Susie, and the drink or two at the Wheatsheaf I'd consoled myself with later that night, I didn't feel too good the next morning, so I lay in bed all day eating bits of bread and cheese, which was all the food I had in the cupboard. I daresay Mrs Fanshawe would have stood me a snack if I'd asked, but after what had happened the previous afternoon I was determined to keep out of her way for a bit. Anyway, the morning after that, which was a Friday, I was feeling myself again, just itching to do the good day's work that would set me up for the weekend. The first thing to do, I told myself, was to go round to Mrs Grayson's and cash in my IOU, so as soon as I'd called in at the office, had a natter with Hastings and collected my kit, I set off back towards Bayswater. The Indian summer was holding up and I was thinking that if I earned enough today I could just about afford to buy Susie a present—an evening bag, say, or a pair of gloves from one of the stores in Regent Street. I'd got this idea, too, for a poem about her and a line or two of that was already sizzling nicely in my head. In sight of Mrs Grayson's, though, I pulled up short. First thing that struck me was that the blinds were down. Second thing was that a bloke in a black suit with a bowler hat on his head was standing on the front step with the door half open behind him.

'Mrs Grayson at home?' I asked him as I twitched open the front gate.

'Mrs Grayson?' He was one of those surly little blokes who take a positive pride in not giving you a straight answer. 'You'll be lucky.'

'Why's that then?'

For an answer he jabbed his thumb in the direction of the street, where there was a black van with *Chas Hamilton & Sons, Funeral Directors* painted on it.

'Dead?'

'Dead as mutton.'

'Anyone about?'

'Bloke that's arranging things is in the house.'

You get all kinds of weird stuff on the door-to-door, but this was the first time I'd had a customer die on me halfway through a transaction.

76

I was sorry about Mrs Grayson; she'd been a nice old girl. Anyhow, I left my kit-bag inside the gate and pressed hard on the door bell. The undertaker's man, meanwhile, had gone to smoke a fag in the street. A middle-aged character with no tie on and big, lugubrious eyes came to the door to see what all the fuss was about. That's the son, most likely, I thought.

'Mr Grayson?'

He looked as if he'd had a few, but you can never tell.

'That's right.'

'My condolences, Mr Grayson, on your sudden loss.'

'Could have happened any time these last ten years,' he said. 'Beats me how she held on as long as she did.'

'Even so.'

'Even so. You a friend of hers?'

'Actually,' I said, 'it was more of a business arrangement.' I handed over the IOU. The way he looked at it made me even more certain he'd had a few.

'Not her writing,' he said finally.

'She gave it to me on this very doorstep not two days ago.'

'I've heard about your sort,' he said. 'Come round robbing them that's grieving for the departed. Think I don't know my own mother's writing? Go on, f—— off.'

He was a big bloke, too, six foot three if he was an inch, so I just nodded my head, civil-like, backed off out of the door, picked up my kit and went off at a brisk pace down the street. Once I'd got twenty yards away, though, I stopped and half-hid myself

77

behind the back of a car. A quarter of an hour or so went by and then I saw him march out of the door in the other direction, hat on head, and clearly not off to the corner shop for a *Mirror*. If you ask me he was headed for the pub. I gave it five minutes and then wandered back. The undertaker's man was sitting in the front of his van reading a paper, which explained why the front door was still open: obviously there was still work to be done. Anyway, I dodged inside, ignored the drawing room and, acting on a hunch I had, took a second right into the kitchen. Sure enough, there were the three lotion bottles sitting on a ledge above the sink. The whole thing took thirty seconds. On the doorstep I met the undertaker's man coming in with a flask of what looked like embalming fluid under his arm.

'F——g awful job, this,' he said. 'Care to swap?'

'I'm a commercial myself,' I said.

'Point taken.' God knows what he thought I was doing.

You'd have thought a start like that would have put the kybosh on the day. Actually it was the other way round: by lunchtime I'd sold half-a-dozen bottles. That was forty-five bob, fifteen bob of which was mine. I was so bucked that I went and had a proper lunch in a pub cut off the joint and two veg with a pint of Pale Ale to wash it down and five Park Drive for afterwards. After this I didn't feel like doing any more work so I hauled the kit back to Holborn on the bus and strolled up to the office where Hastings was reading a copy of *The Story of San Michele*.

'You're back early,' he said.

I told him about Mrs Grayson and the IOU.

'I've known queerer things than that,' Hastings

78

said.

'You remember when those newfangled coffee pots—percolators—were coming in a few years back? I was up north in those days, Manchester way. There must have been a dozen firms selling them. Got so's you couldn't move for coffee pots. Anyway, I sold one to an old girl once—big house in Didsbury, maid to answer the door—and when she opened the cupboard to stow it away there was a shelf full of them already. Same brand, too. That reminds me,' he said. 'Got something for you.'

And he handed me a little brass paperweight, on which had been engraved the words: *Abraxas Carpet Cleaning Co. Salesman of the Month: J. Ross.*

'Even beat old Callender,' he said. Something else struck him and he went on: 'Public school man aren't you?'

'St Paul's,' I admitted.

'Thought you were. Can always tell. I was at Marlborough myself.'

Truth to tell, I wasn't surprised by this. Life's full of dark horses. I once queued up at the Labour with a chap who said he was an earl's grandson. Even so, it must have been a bit of a come-down for an old Marlborough man to be running the Abraxas Carpet Cleaning Co. from a dirty table in Holborn.

'Don't mind my asking . . .' I said, seeing that he quite wanted to be asked. 'But how'd you end up here?'

'Point taken,' he said, like the undertaker. 'Drink mostly. You'll be too young to have been in the war?'

I told him about the clerking job steaming open envelopes at Southern Command.

'I had charge of a mule camp round the back

of Arras,' he said. 'Nothing to do except keep the numbers up and get the shit shovelled away. That's what did it.'

'How's Mr Roper?' I asked.

'Bad. I went to see him the other day and he thought there were spiders crawling out of the lino. Thing is, what with us being short-staffed, there's a supervisor's job going. Four quid a week. Think about it.'

Another bloke came into the office just then complaining about a bottle of lotion that had been mixed too strong and taken off the top layer of someone's parquet, so I slung my hook. I was flattered, in spite of myself. *Supervisor, Abraxas Carpet Cleaning Co.* Of course, I wasn't going to take it, but the old lady would have been impressed.

Anyhow, I was in an A1 mood as I trekked my way back to Paddington. I had fifteen bob in my jacket pocket, which, together with what I could rake in next morning, meant the weekend ought to go OK. Tomorrow lunchtime I'd go down to the City Road and see if I couldn't meet Susie out of work and who knows what we wouldn't do? I was still thinking about this, and smoking one of the Park Drive I'd bought, when I turned the corner along from Ma Fanshawe's and found a little chap waiting by the gate. Now, I know trouble when I see it and this one had it with a capital T. He was wearing a mac and a trilby hat and there was a fat briefcase wedged under his arm, but what you really noticed were his eyes, which darted all over the place like fish in a tank. At the very least he was a bailiff or a dun. As I made to turn in at the gate, he stood slightly to one side.

'Your name Ross?'

'Could be.'

'James Ross of 24 Sispara Gardens W2?'

When I nodded he tossed me a slip of paper from out of the breast pocket of his suit. 'You'll be wanting this then?'

And would you believe it, it was the letter I'd sent to the old lady, the one about Mrs Keach and the younger set. Like an idiot I must have put it in the same envelope as the one to West End Central. There was a second or so's silence while I digested this and the little chap enjoyed the spectacle of me doing it.

'You the police?'

'Never you mind who I am,' he said. 'You and me need to have a chat.'

There was a pub halfway down Sispara Gardens on the other side and we ended up there with a half-pint of mild and bitter apiece. The little chap sipped his fondly. 'Not often I get to drink on the job,' he said. 'My name's Haversham. Any time you want to talk to me, you can ring this number.' And he flipped over a square of card with a telephone number written on it in pencil. 'Now, how'd you come across this fellow Rasmussen?'

'Girl I know works in his office.'

'That's the ticket. Been there much?'

'Just the once.'

'See anything?'

'Not much to see.'

'Mm-hm. Thing is,' said Haversham—the insides of his fingers were stained dark brown with tobacco—'we've had our eye on this character Rasmussen—McTavish, whatever his name is—for quite some time. Interesting bloke. Spends half his time in Mayfair as far as I can see, hobbing with the nobs. Daresay that's where he gets his tips. Nothing to go on, though. No chance of a search warrant or anything. That's where you come in.'

'How's that then?'

'If your young lady works in his office, you can come up with a way of getting in there again and having a look-see.'

'What if I don't want to?'

'All right, let's put it another way. What line of work you in son?'

'Door-to-door.'

'Mm-hm. Commission job, eh? Paid in cash, I s'pose? Well, that might be worth me looking into for a start. Get the idea?' he said.

I got the idea.

'That's the spirit,' he said. He had an odd, mad look in his eyes that I'd seen once or twice before in blokes who'd wangled their way into some kind of official job, and I didn't like it above half. 'Number's on the card. Don't worry. Not expecting you to find the crown jewels in a paper bag. But if I don't hear anything in a fortnight or so, I daresay you'll find me this way again.'

Outside the rain had come on again and there were people with umbrellas drifting home in the twilight, lights going on in front rooms, gates swinging where their owners had forgotten to kick them shut. I watched him traipse off down Sispara Gardens, leaving a little spurt of cigarette smoke trailing in the air as he went. Back in the house, Mrs Fanshawe was boiling a ham in the basement and the smell came halfway up the staircase. Usually I went to the Wheatsheaf on a Friday night. This time, though, I decided to stay at home. There were things I needed to think about.

7

WHITE CITY

8 p.m. 440 yds pursuit, Caragh Cup. 2–1 Danish Flyer, 5–2 Likely Lad, 4–1 Door Knocker, 5–1 Bar the Field

He came out of the station into a blaze of artificial light. There was a sign on the brick wall that said *Stadium 400 yards* with a thick black arrow stencilled beneath and he set off automatically round the knots of people collected on the station steps and out into the street. Here the light wasn't so flaring and there were cars heading north, hooting at the crowd that every so often spilled off the pavement and into the road. Christ! There must be a couple of hundred people making their way up to Wood Lane. You got all sorts at the dogs. Tough-looking blokes with racing papers under their elbows. Tarts who wouldn't know one end of a dog from the other. Old women with bits of knitting sticking out of the tops of their handbags. He watched as a gang of girls in sailor hats and cheap, shiny skirts came shrieking past and curled his lip. Kind of borassics who ought to be at home minding their kid sisters, not down the dog track.

Falling in with the crowd, and steering a passage with his elbows, he allowed himself to be carried on to the stadium, noting as he did so the ever-growing mass of people gathered inside the turnstiles. F——g thousands of them, there were. How was he ever going to find the Bloke in all that? 'White City,

83

Wednesday night,' Davenport had said. 'That's where he'll be. Likes a flutter on the f——g dogs, he does. You take my word for it.' He'd just have to hang about and chance his luck, that was all. And maybe have a flutter himself, too, if he felt like it. There was a quid in his pocket. You could go a long way at the dogs with a quid. He milled around in the crowd for a bit, staring hard at the women and even harder at the men with them who stared back, and paid threepence for a programme, all the while looking out across the stadium and the farther side of the track for his real quarry. Christ! He was thirsty, too. Plenty of bars, but what he could really do with was a cup of the old ackamaracke. He paid another sixpence for a pie and started eating it jammed up against a wall with his face in the shadow, next to a courting couple talking about which dogs they were going to back.

White City stadium. Cor! He'd been here when he was a kid, breaking in through an old fence round the back and looking for betting slips people had chucked away. It was different now. Moving out of the shadow the male half of the courting couple had got his hand inside the girl's coat, which was quick work—he tried to take stock of his surroundings: the towering arc of the stands, the huge gantries beyond, light shining off the windows of the lounges and boxes in the upper tiers, the dun-coloured oval of the track. There were dogs out in the exercise area and he went to take a look.

He knew a bit about greyhounds, enough to understand that you stayed clear of them in all but exceptional circumstances, but still . . . Resting his elbows on the lip of the fence he saw a man loiter up to a black dog with a muzzle round its jaw and,

84

in the guise of patting it, surreptitiously administer a pinch to its hock. Well, that was one not to back, wasn't it? The pie had stuck halfway down his gut and was making him feel queasy. If he was the Bloke, come to the White City, where would he go? Down by the track-side or up in one of the bars? He walked further along the perimeter fence to a space where half-a-dozen bookies had their stands. *Chas Fuller, Hoxton. Jas Porter. The Old Firm. All bets paid.* There were tic-tac boys out signalling to their mates over in the half-dollar enclosure, and he stopped to watch them, thinking that they were laying off bets and he might get a tip. He'd had a pal who'd been a tic-tac boy and knew something about it. A biggish feller, about his own age, was standing a few feet away and he watched the play of his hands. Three taps on the shoulder. That meant the dog in lane three. Fists banged together once. Christ! That meant someone had dropped half a ton. No wonder the bookie was so keen to lay it off. He opened the programme and checked the dog's name, took a ten-shilling note out of his pocket and went up to the bookie furthest away from the tic-tac boy.

'Ten bob on Satan's Pride, mate?'

'Ere y'are son.'

He got odds of four to one. That would do nicely. Meanwhile, the bookie whose tic-tac boy had been signalling had wiped Satan's Pride's name off his slate.

All this time he was surveying the crowd, looking for the Bloke. No sign of him though. Jewish-looking men in fur coats with fat women on their arms went by and he glanced at them contemptuously. F——g yids, lallying around as if they owned the place. It had started to rain and he pulled up the collar of his coat. The race was about to start and he stood on tiptoe so that he could see the dogs being put in their cages. Christ! Satan's Pride didn't look up to much. Kind of dog you could see being chased by a whippet in the park. There was a bang and the hare jerked and came whizzing out of its trap with the dogs loping behind. A pale brown dog with mad eyes was making the running. One of the other dogs had stopped and was licking its paw. Satan's Pride was well down. He was about to turn away in disgust when the crowd next to the track-side set up a roar and he saw that Satan's Pride was putting it on. Well, how about that? Won by a length. That was two quid, less tax.

Casually—just so people would know he wasn't one of those mugs who went steaming over to the bookies every time they won sixpence—he went over to collect his winnings. Five yards away a big man with what looked like a razor scar down one side of his face was stuffing Bradburys into his wallet. No prizes for guessing who'd put on the half a ton, then. For an instant his two quid seemed faintly pitiful to him, but then his spirits rose again. Two quid! That was a bit of backsheesh all right. He'd have a drink on the strength of that, and not in one of the cheap places either. At the back of the stand there was a sign that said 'Lounge Bar' and he ploughed on through the door, ignoring the glance of the uniformed commissionaire on the topmost step. It was full of men in suits with expensive-looking women sitting at rows of little two-seater tables. He ordered a double Bells—that was the stuff—and drank it neat, standing with one foot on the chromium rail and one eye on the barmaid, who was so well stacked you wondered how she could stand up straight, and then looked to see if they had any cigars. He was so preoccupied with his success and the taste of the whisky at the back of his mouth—that was the stuff all right— and the barmaid's tits heaving about like f——g blancmange that he didn't notice the Bloke. But there he was, parked in a kind of alcove towards the back with a bottle of something in front of him and another bloke and a couple of women on either side. Real lookers the women were, too, not like some of the tarts who made it into the lounge just because their old man had had a lucky morning selling jargoons in Bethnal Green.

He drank some more of the whisky while he wondered what to do. He didn't think the Bloke had seen him. What he wanted was to get the Bloke on his own. Well, he could do that, couldn't he, if he played his cards right? Carefully positioning himself with his back towards the alcove, he strained to hear what they were saying, but the Bloke was talking in an undertone and the woman on his near side had one of those syrupy, la-di-dah voices that went *My dear we had simply the most unbelievable time, o really how could you think such a thing* and in the end he gave up. They had some cigars. He got the barmaid to bring him one and stared hard at her blouse as she brought it. A bob it cost. Nice smoking a cigar. He could see out of the corner of his eye that the Bloke was smoking one. Drinking up the remainder of the whisky, he moved back towards the doorway of the lounge and out onto the steps. The commissionaire, bouncing up at his elbow and remembering him from before, said:

'Can't stand there, sir.'

87

'Why not?'

'Blocks up the steps sir, and the people can't get out.'

'Ain't no f——g people trying to get out, as far as I can see.'

'I'll thank you not to use language like that, sir.'

'Oh f—— off.'

There was a copper twenty yards away under the lights, but the commissionaire hadn't seen him, so he dodged back down towards the track, all the time keeping his eyes on the door of the lounge. At some point the Bloke would have to come out, wouldn't he? And then he'd be there.

They were bawling the dogs in for another race, but he took no notice. Stop when you were ahead, that was the way. The cigar was finished now and he needed something else to smoke, but he knew that if he went off to buy fags from the kiosk he'd lose his vantage point. Another few minutes went by. He stared disinterestedly at the people who milled round him. Mugs, all of them. Blokes who couldn't say boo to a goose. Silly tarts who hung on their arms and thought about the sofa they'd got from Drages on the HP and reckoned they'd done well for themselves. Gah! For some reason the memory of that morning in the Caledonian Road ran through his head and he remembered the pale girl sitting up in bed smoking one of his cigarettes with the sheet pulled up to her chest, but not so far as he couldn't see what was underneath it. The dogs started off round the track and the crowd stirred and the announcer's voice crackled over the roar to say that Limehouse Boy was in the lead from Victory March. There were people coming out of the lounge, a woman tugging a fox fur over her shoulder, a man with a tall hat—a real toff, you didn't get many of them here and he looked to see if the Bloke was with them. F—— it, his luck was in. Four people coming down the walk way with the crowd bellowing their approval of Limehouse Boy, and the Bloke was one of them. One of the women looked like his secretary, but he couldn't be sure at this distance. As they came level with him he ducked into the mass of people by the track-side and collided with a burly man in a bowler hat.

'Why don't you watch where you're f——g going, son?'

'Why don't you f——g watch yourself, you Berkshire?'

The Bloke and his party were heading off towards the main gate. He fell in behind them, ten yards away. Just let the Bloke end up on his own and he'd show him. Have that ten quid faster than Gene Tunney's arm going in. All these people crowding him. Why couldn't they get out of his way? He could see the girl sitting up in the bed again, and the filthy sheet. Why hadn't he hung about, eh, instead of lallying off to Finsbury Pavement like that?

He was eight yards away now, seven, the crowd parting in deference to his unspoken wish. The people in the stands—mugs—were still cheering for Limehouse Boy. He'd been to Limehouse once when he was skint and kipped in a place that cost sevenpence, and would have cost nothing if he'd climbed in with the deputy. Catch him at that game, though. The deputy had had a cast in one eye and a funny little faraway voice. They were in sight of the gate now and there were official-looking blokes in dark jackets hanging about and a copper parked by one of the coffee stalls. Couldn't do anything there. He pulled the collar of his coat up to his chin again. Another roar from the stand behind him broke over his head. Beyond the gate he kept the Bloke and his party in his sights. They were standing together under a street lamp talking excitedly. At least the la-di-dah woman was—*o my dear how too amusing, I can't think when I last*—while the Bloke and his mate looked on. Couple of mugs. Then out of nowhere a car chugged up—a real flash one, an Armstrong-Siddeley, with a chauffeur in a peaked cap at the wheel and his heart sank. What if they all just got in it and drove away? But no, it was only the other feller and the women who were climbing aboard.

The Bloke stood waving them off with his fingers up to the brim of his hat. A quarter of a mile distant he could see the lights of the Underground winking up through the murk. There was no one much about. He was only five yards away now. As he stole nearer a policeman came out of the shadows beyond the arc of street light and sauntered flat-footedly by. Christ! That was all he needed. Surely the copper would be off back to the police station? There was one back down the road, he knew, near the Scrubs. No? Well, he'd just have to plod along behind and see how things turned out. He took a sight on the back of the Bloke's collar and went on, trying not to look conspicuous. Then, just as they got to the mouth of the tube, a gang of people surged up from the other side of the road and he lost sight of him. He tried to push on but it was no good. They were all jammed up against the wall and the copper was hollering for people to slow down. Gah!

He stood looking wildly about through the throng, but there was no one there. Another evening down the can. Still, he told himself, there was that two quid in his pocket to add to the one he already had. As he stood there uncertainly, wondering what to do, a girl in a battered felt hat with lipstick smudging down the side of her cheek came up and said:

'You got a cigarette you can spare?'

He peered at her through the haze of orange light. 'What?'

'I said: you got a cigarette you can spare?'

'No.' A thought struck him. 'Can get you a packet, though, if you want.'

She was about eighteen, he thought, with lumps of badly applied face powder that failed to disguise the suety skin beneath. There was a kiosk over in the entrance hall's farther side. He took her arm and began to propel her firmly towards it.

8
PRIMROSE PATHS

Sound advice for the Salesman: IV. Audacity

We all know the salesman who plods dutifully from one customer to the next, who is content with modest returns and will never, in that time-honoured phrase, 'set the Thames on fire.' Such men are to be avoided, for the true salesman is not found among their ranks. Remember—audacity and brashness are not the same thing, and that a customer who disdains a display of breast-beating may be won over by an apposite remark. Sometimes a successful sale may require a bold approach. But be warned! Faint heart never won full order book. The successful salesman is the one who focuses his attention not on the customer, or on the product, but on the sale!

Abraxas Salesman's Handbook

'So the company commander said: "If I don't get an explanation for the irregularities in these mess accounts on my desk by tomorrow morning there's men here that'll be losing a pip." And just as he said it a whizz-bang came flying over—we were only a couple of miles behind the lines, you understand—and crashed right into the stockyard.'

'What happened?'

'What happened? Half of it was blown to buggery. I spent the next three hours shovelling up mule guts in a pail.'

'No, I mean what happened about the mess accounts?'

'Now that was the interesting thing. Turned out it was the company commander that had been fiddling them himself to take some voluntary-aid nurse he was carrying on with at the military hospital to Paris for the weekend.'

It was towards the end of a Friday forenoon and I was sitting in the office at Doughty Street listening to Hastings prosing on about his time in the army. In normal circumstances I'd have been knocking on doors in Bayswater, which was still proving a pretty good beat, but Hastings was a decent bloke and I didn't mind humouring him. He was obviously desperate to talk to someone and it might as well be me. Since Roper's DTs would apparently be keeping him in hospital for a good long time, Hastings had been promoted to full supervisor, which meant he was a good man to keep in with.

'Of course,' he said, lighting what I reckoned was the seventh fag of the last twenty minutes, 'you were in that show yourself. I quite forgot. Southern Command wasn't it?'

So I explained again about the little hut halfway up the downs where a lance-corporal and I sat steaming open the mail and seeing if there was any mention of the geography of Vimy Ridge or what Haig had said to Alexander that morning at breakfast, which there never was: it was all just smut.

'You know,' Hastings said gloomily, as if it had only just occurred to him, 'I always think that was where my life started going wrong.'

Above our heads someone was vacuuming the

staircase. They never used the carpet lotion for this, I'd noticed, always a vacuum cleaner. Fact is, I wasn't feeling too bad that morning. For one thing I was meeting Susie for lunch somewhere near City Road. And after that I aimed to pay a call on a chap I knew in Bloomsbury who'd just been made editor of a literary magazine, so the afternoon wasn't shaping up too badly at all.

'You married?' Hastings asked suddenly. He had this habit of changing the tilt of a conversation in unexpected ways.

'Nearly was once.' I told him about Netta and the time she'd thrown the ring at me in the cinema queue.

Hastings looked grave. 'Women are funny cattle,' he said. 'Now, take my wife . . .' Hastings, I knew—we'd got quite matey by this time—lived up west somewhere and had two kids. I was bracing myself for something on the warm side, but he thought better of it, stared hard at the calendar on the wall by his desk, which was a couple of months out of date, and then started off in another direction.

'You seen Callender lately?'

'Not to speak of.' It was true as well. I'd been keeping out of his way and he'd been keeping out of mine, though one of the other blokes had told me he was working a terrific fiddle down in Kensington now, subcontracting the work and running a team of salesmen that Hastings didn't know about. 'Problem is there?' I asked.

'Don't know as you'd call it a problem. Still sells plenty of stuff. More, if it comes to that. Five pound seventeen and six last week alone. It's just that I never set eyes on him. Sends kids in here with notes asking for bottles. Money, too, sometimes. I can't

94

understand it.'

I wondered whether to let him in on Callender's secret, but decided against it: it was none of my business and Callender wouldn't thank me for it if he found out. Besides, between you and me, there was something a bit depressing about the Abraxas Carpet Cleaning Co. these days. The old blokes who'd hung about in the basement canteen eating rock buns and talking about their livers had mostly gone now, and I didn't altogether care for their replacements: they were young chaps, younger than me, who never gave you the time of day. Worse, the atmosphere of the place was turning definitely seedy. The dead bluebottles sunning themselves on the table inside the front door had been there all summer, and the top-most copy of the pile of salesman's handbooks on the edge of Hasting's desk had a film of dust on it a quarter of an inch thick. I've been in enough dodgy outfits in my time to know when trouble's brewing and it seemed to me that Abraxas was properly on the slide.

'Well, I'd best be going now,' I said, picking up my hat from off my knee and sticking it on my head. 'Got a chap to see. Actually'—I'd just remembered the real reason I'd dropped in the office that morning—'you couldn't let me have that seven and six, could you?'

'There's only a tenner in the cash-box. Be going to the bank this afternoon.'

And that was another thing about Abraxas these days: shortage of ready money. There'd even been talk of paying some of the commission by cheque, which is a sure sign that the wind is up. Anyway, I told him I might call by later in the afternoon— Bloomsbury, where I was heading to see my

95

pal, Jimmy, was nearby anyhow—and I breezed off along the corridor to the front door, leaving Hastings to light fag number eleven. On the way out I nipped into the gents, where the porcelain tiling sported several additions. Next to *you don't have to be mad to work here but it helps* someone had written *detective smith knows how to gee, tell him he's a c—— from me*, which I thought rather odd, but there you are. Outside in the street the sun was up and a file of oriental types in suits were filing into the Dickens Museum, being harangued by an old party with a beard and a tarboosh as they went. I was more interested, though, in the little bloke parked on the other side of the street with a folded mac over his arm and that morning's *Express* held up close to his face, but not so close that his eyes didn't show above the top of the page. It wasn't Haversham, but it could easily have been Haversham's long-lost cousin. Anyway, before I knew what I was doing I was halfway over the road and making a beeline for him.

'Got a light?'

'No.' He was still looking over my shoulder at the front steps I'd just descended.

'Lend us sixpence then?'

'F—— off.'

I took the hint, but at least I'd established it wasn't me he was after. The last thing I wanted was Haversham or any of his chums hanging round the office. By now it was about half-past twelve, so I headed south to the Clerkenwell Road and then went east in the direction of Old Street. The reason I'd decided to walk wasn't just to save money on the bus fare, but because I could feel the restlessness surging up in me again. It was queer, because I hadn't had the restless feeling for a while—not since the time with Netta, in fact, when I was selling vacuum cleaners on the coast. I reckoned it was to do with Susie and the job and Hastings' long, gloomy face staring up at me through the haze of cigarette smoke. He was a decent bloke, Hastings, but he was no advertisement for turning forty, or steady employment, or the comforts of hearth and home, and all those other things we're supposed to be longing for. All this set me thinking about what I really wanted out of life—it's odd how this stuff gets into your head, but there you are—and I decided that, really, it was only Susie and the writing. I had this vision of the two of us staying in a cottage: Hampshire, say, near enough to London for the odd trip to the Wheatsheaf, far enough away for quiet, with me scribbling away and Susie . . . well, I had this picture of Susie sitting on a deckchair in the garden with a hat and pair of Lido trousers, so you can imagine how I envisaged the whole thing.

I got to the Lyons we'd agreed to meet in at one o'clock on the dot, but there was no sign of her so I told the nippie to bring me a glass of milk and a bun. While I waited I looked around the room, which was full of dreadful old dug-outs—clerks from the big offices eating Welsh rarebits or staring mournfully at their plates of kippers, and girls in twos and threes shrieking over what the boss had said to them that morning. Just wait until you're my age, I thought, and see if things are such a treat. There was still no sign of her—it was ten past one now and I'd finished the milk and the bun—so I dived into a paper someone had left on the high stool next to me, read the sports news and a highbrow leader about Mr Snowden, browsed

97

through an account of a party given by someone called Mrs Pilkington-Withers and finally fetched up at the horoscope. Under 'Leo' it said: *Your chief fault is your modesty. In love you will find that the primrose path to happiness is unusually complicated. Seize every opportunity the day offers you!*

Not that bad, I thought, regretting all that modesty, which had been my undoing, but it set me thinking about how odd it was being fixed up with Susie, her not being my type in the least. Usually, you see, I fall hook, line and sinker for those incredibly beautiful but sulky girls—the sort who, 1,000 years ago, would have had wars fought over them and enjoyed watching their lovers slaughter each other on their behalf—whereas Susie was one of those bright, bouncy creatures of the kind you see in adverts, hiking all day on a slab of Vitamalt. She liked me, too, whereas the incredibly beautiful but sulky types would just about condescend to be stood dinner provided there were no hot hands under the table. It was eighteen minutes past one and the nippie was watching the stool I'd kept empty. I was wondering whether I shouldn't step down to the office to see where she was when suddenly she sat down beside me, hefting her shopping back into the space between our feet and sending a great gust of warm, lavender-scented air in my direction.

'I'm sorry I'm late,' she said. 'I had to stay and type a letter for Mr Rasmussen before he went out to lunch.'

'Oh yes,' I said, conscious of my new responsibilities. 'What's he been keeping you busy at then?'

She was looking a bit amused, but I couldn't

get anything out of her until the nippie had sailed in and we'd ordered a couple of poached eggs on toast apiece. Then she said: 'Oh, he's moving in High Society these days. I've to write his thank-you letters.'

'What sort of High Society?'

'Well, have you ever heard of a place called Newcome Grange?'

I'd come across this in one of the gossip columns. 'Isn't that where Mrs Antrobus lives?'

'That's the one. The one who had the Prince of Wales to her iced coffee party. Well, he's been asked there for the weekend.'

Just the kind of thing Haversham would be interested in, I thought, but she didn't seem as keen on telling me about it as I was to hear about it, and pretty soon we were back on the usual treadmill of what we'd been doing in each other's absence. My activities had amounted to selling carpet lotion and thinking of her, but I couldn't very well tell her that, so I improvised a couple of evenings at the Wheatsheaf among the writers and a trip to the cinema—a solitary visit, I was at pains to emphasize—to see Jack Oakie in *Let's Go Native*.

'You're looking very smart,' I said. And she was, in one of those crisp, white blouses that have embroidery over the neck and cuffs and a skirt that showed off her legs. 'How's your friend Gladys?'

She looked a bit puzzled. 'Gladys?'

'The one whose young man had gone to Leeds and was seeing a girl in a tobacconist's shop.'

'Oh, I haven't heard from her just lately.'

This struck me as odd, for ever since I'd known her Susie had prosed on endlessly about Gladys and her young man, who, to judge from what was said

99

about Gladys, was well out of it.

'Tell you what,' I said, as she applied herself to her poached eggs. 'I've an idea.'

'What sort of an idea?'

I took a deep breath. The scheme had been floating about in my head for a week or so now. Its execution depended on her liking it and me being able to afford it. I was pretty confident about the second bit, less so about the first.

'Why don't we go away for the weekend somewhere?'

'Where to exactly?'

I'd thought about this. 'In the country maybe. A room at a pub. Or a cottage somewhere.'

She thought about this with her fork held halfway to her mouth. Suddenly I found myself wondering about all kinds of things to do with her that I'd never previously considered: who her parents were; what kind of pictures she liked; whether Susie was short for Susan or Suzanne. The Lyons was clearing now, and the bright sunshine flooded through the door in a wash. The old lawyers' clerks had gone back to their desks in Finsbury Square and Bunhill Row and the shrieking girls had disappeared.

'Actually,' she said, 'I'm a bit tied up at the moment.'

'What about in a fortnight's time? We'll go somewhere nice. Promise.'

'That's when we're staying at Newcome Grange.'

'We?'

'Mr Rasmussen's very busy. He wants me to go with him in case anything comes up.'

'I don't believe you.'

'It's true,' she said. 'And it's very rude of you not to believe me. He's got the gramophone business

100

now in Holborn and there's a lot of work on.'

I saw how it was then: I was being given the run-around. Somehow this always happened with women, even with Mrs Bence-Jones, who'd had pince-nez and teeth that stuck out at forty-five degree angles. Always there came that moment when they remembered the existence of long-lost aunts they just had to spend Saturday afternoon with, or the best friend up in town for the weekend who had to be taken out and shown the sights. There was something almost dutiful about this, I'd noticed, as if they'd all read some book about how you were supposed to behave to men, like a game of chess in which you let all his pawns march up the board for a bit before letting rip with the big pieces held in reserve.

All I could do was to make the best of a bad job, which was another lunch date in the middle of next week, but after this she said she had to go as Mr Rasmussen would be back from lunch and wanting to give her some more letters to type, and I watched her sail off into the street and past the window, waving as she went. All this had knocked the cheery thoughts I'd been thinking in Hastings' office clean out of my head, and I sat there for a minute or two reflecting that it had been a queer couple of weeks, what with Mrs Grayson dying and the appearance of Haversham and now Susie turning out to be everywoman after all. It was about two o'clock now—it occurred to me that Mr Rasmussen must take extraordinarily short lunch hours so I decided I'd head off towards Bloomsbury and try looking up my pal Jimmy. As I went I sketched out the first paragraph of a letter I reckoned I might write that evening to Susie, all about the things I felt about her and the way she was treating me. It wasn't half bad, I thought, but I knew, deep down, that I wouldn't send it.

As I marched on westward from the City, and the memory of the lunch date began to fade, I felt a bit better. Fact is, I was looking forward no end to seeing my pal Jimmy who, unlike most of the people I've knocked about with since the war, had really landed on his feet. The *Blue Bugloss*, which he'd just become editor of, was as swanky as they come: issued monthly in pink-and-blue board covers, owned by some City type who reckoned that by subsidizing it he was paying off his debt to culture, it simply dripped with intellectual sophistication. When I'd rung up the other day to speak to Jimmy the phone had been answered by a girl who sounded as though she'd been at Roedean and who told me that 'Mr Carstairs' was unavailable. All of which, needless to say, was a big leg-up for Jimmy, who when I'd first known him was making a living compiling the 'Brain-brighteners' for *Tit-bits*.

Anyway, the *Blue Bugloss*'s offices were in one of those wide squares to the east of Gower Street that look as if they're 1,000 miles away from London, with big, tree-lined gardens full of kids playing hopscotch and skirmishing through the bushes. All this cheered me up no end—the magazines that mostly published my stuff operated from garrets at the wrong end of Chelsea. When I'd had enough of looking at the square I had myself buzzed up by reception to a big, carpeted landing where a toney-looking secretary bobbed past with a file under her arm. Jimmy was waiting to take me off to his room. Do you know those offices in the

Bloomsbury squares, I wonder? This one had a view out over the plane trees, and a big deal table that Jimmy, who was on the compact side, looked swamped behind. On the wall there was a signed photo of John Galsworthy and a picture of the founding editor, a wild-eyed old boy with a beard like a furze bush. Jimmy, I noticed, looked pleased to see me but a bit subdued. Perhaps the girls from Roedean were getting him down.

'Nice billet,' I said, truthfully.

'It's not so bad. Do you know,' he said—he sounded a bit conspiratorial—'somebody told me Osbert Sitwell applied for this job?'

'So how did you get it?'

'They wanted a younger man.'

There were some new books on the table— review copies sent in by publishers in flimsy paper dust-jackets and I picked up one of them and turned the pages beneath my fingers.

'You can't have that,' he said. 'I've promised that to Cyril.'

'Fair enough. Can I send you some stuff then? A poem, say?'

'Be my guest. It'll make a change from some of the things that get sent in.' He held up a sheet of paper from the litter on his desk.

'Listen to this:

Where is this stream, the crystal of my sadness,
the luminous, fallen statue of despair?
The stream, the purest portrait of my madness
and the ruby blossom, above all my dead, burning
the deep, dark air?

'Who's the lucky man?' I asked.

'Brian someone. One of the Oxford lot.'

'Shall you print it?'

'Don't see why not.'

I was looking over the strew of paper—invites to literary 'at homes', catalogues for an exhibition of primitive art someone was holding somewhere, all the rubbish you get in an editor's office—when my eye fell on something that pulled me up with a start. It was a typed letter, sent by a secretary I suppose, from an address in Lowndes Square, wondering if Mr James Carstairs would give Mrs Bertha Antrobus the pleasure of joining her for a few days at her country residence at Newcome Grange, Sussex.

'Looks like another nice billet,' I said, holding it up and trying not to sound too interested. 'Who's Mrs Antrobus?'

'That society woman. Never met her in my life, but she's just nuts about culture apparently. Maltravers knows her.'

Maltravers was the *Blue Bugloss*'s proprietor. I'd seen him once at a party. He was about my age, too, f—— him.

'Shall you be going?'

'Working in offices with girls who I always think are going to ask me if I'd mind planting out the begonias is one thing,' Jimmy said, 'but I draw the line at country house weekends. Look, just excuse me a tick will you?'

While he was out of the room I reflected briefly on the moral implications of what I was about to do, discounted them, picked up the letter and stuffed it into the pocket of my jacket, carefully sifting the piles of paper into a passable imitation of the previous chaos. My heart was banging away behind my ribs but I figured it was too good a chance to miss. I could keep an eye on Rasmussen, which would please Haversham, plus I'd be in the house with Susie.

When Jimmy came back I had my nose deep in the review copy.

'Actually,' Jimmy said, 'you can have that. I've just remembered that Cyril said he was going to Toulon with Eddie and Johnny Bant.'

'Thanks very much.'

'They say Johnny Bant's got the clap,' Jimmy volunteered, 'but I don't suppose Cyril will mind.'

Out on the landing we bumped into the good-looking girl who'd come bobbing past when I'd arrived, and Jimmy said: 'This is Mr Ross, Merope. He's going to be sending us in a great deal of material over the next few months, so make sure you look out for it.'

'Yes, Mr Carstairs.'

As I've said before, there's nothing like a good education for teaching you how to put people in their place.

*   *   *

You'd have thought I'd had enough excitement for one day. As it turned out there were a couple more surprises in store. On the way back to Doughty Street—I didn't see why I should let seven-and-six stand over until Monday—I was already thinking about the weekend at Newcome Grange. The more I thought about it the more I realized it wasn't as far-fetched as I'd imagined. She'd never set eyes on me or Jimmy. And if there was anyone else there who had—unlikely, I reckoned—I could simply make my excuses and leave. As far as I knew, there wasn't any law against impersonating people, and it wasn't as if I stood to gain financially. It would take a bit of cheek, but I fancied the rewards would be worth the winning. Anyway, I'd bucked up no end by the time I'd got to Doughty Street, with the book Jimmy had given me wedged under my arm and Mrs Antrobus's invite tucked in my jacket. It was one of those slow mid-afternoons when the streets turn suddenly empty of traffic, with just a leaf or two blowing gently over the pavement. I'd collected my three half-crowns off Hastings, who'd clearly been out for one or two in my absence, and was hanging about in the hallway when there was a noise of footsteps somewhere below and Callender came slouching up from the basement. He had a fat cigar in his mouth and a couple of oranges in the palm of one hand, and looked even more pleased with himself than usual.

'Can't go wrong with second favourites,' he said, by way of explanation. 'Cleared three quid this morning off the bookie in Cowcross Street. Want one of these?'

I thought he was offering me a cigar, but it turned out that he meant the oranges, so I shook my head.

'Suit yourself,' Callender said. He looked more than ever like one of the gravediggers in *Hamlet*. 'Glad I seen you,' he went on. But why he was glad to see me I never found out, because the very next second the street door flew open and a vague scuffling noise I'd heard on the steps gave way to a pair of coppers and the little man I'd seen hanging around that morning. It took me a moment to work out what was going on, but it was clearly Callender

106

they were after, for when he saw them he gave a kind of whoop of derision and hared off up the staircase behind him with the oranges bouncing down over the treads as he ran. God knows what he thought he was going to do—jump out of a window or shin down the drainpipe most likely—but the first of the coppers got him with a rugger tackle before he was halfway up, and that was that: Callender, with his tie twisted up round his neck, and the two coppers breathing heavily, and the little bloke in the mac turning out Callender's pockets—I didn't see anything except a roll of notes and some betting slips—and a terrible stink of cigar smoke and orange pulp: one of the coppers had trodden on an orange, you see, as he rushed up the stairs.

'Detective f——g Smith ain't it?' was all Callender said as they hauled him away—there was a police van out in the street, I could see—but he gave me a wink, which I hope Detective Smith, if that was his name, didn't notice. I wondered if this had anything to do with Hastings, but there was no sound from his office and so I stood in the hallway listening to the van rev up and Callender saying something to the coppers as they loaded him into it. The whole thing had taken about ninety seconds, and put the wind up me no end.

Still, though, that wasn't all. After I'd watched Callender being arrested I mooched around the West End until opening time, thinking that I'd go and have a couple with some convivial company in the Wheatsheaf. But it was early days for the literary crowd, and there was only Parkinson with his tongue hanging out for a free drink, so after a while I headed back to Ma Fanshawe's. It was a mild night, full of girls standing at bus stops waiting for their young men, and I hadn't felt so low in ages. But then, propped up against my door with another note from Mrs Fanshawe saying that £3.15s was owing, I found a letter that must have come by the early evening post.

Dear James,

It was very kind of you to ask me to go away with you for the weekend and I should very much like to. Hoping that we can be together very soon.
With love from
Susie

Well, what do you know? I wasn't being given the runaround after all.

PART TWO

PART TWO

9

BRIGHTON BELLE

Sound Advice for the Salesman: V. Leisure

*Not even the most persistent salesman can
apply himself continuously to his task. All work
and no play, as the saying goes, makes Jack a
dull boy. Even the most zealous operator, the
really tip-top man, esteemed by his superiors
and admired by those without his pertinacity,
will find that he benefits from 'taking a break',
allowing himself a change of scene and the
opportunity to relax a crowded and over-stressed
mind. At the same time, the canny salesman
is the one who makes use of his leisure.
Half-a-dozen sound ideas, hatched in the
quiet of a summer beach, will enable him to
return to his labours with a distinct competitive
advantage—that ever-coveted 'edge' which
separates the live-wire from the drone and the
future executive from the disposable also-ran.*

Abraxas Salesman's Handbook

And then something odd happened. Not as odd
as the Sunday morning the CO dropped dead on
Church Parade twenty minutes after promising to
put my name in for a commission, but definitely out
of the normal run of things. Coming home from
work one night—I'd been up West Hampstead way
trying some of those big new apartment blocks—I

found a letter from Tommy Kilmarnock propped up against the door, asking me to come round to his chambers first thing the next morning. I don't think I've told you about Tommy Kilmarnock, but he was the only person I'd ever knocked around with—the possible exception being Jimmy—who could properly be called a success. Just now he was working as a high-class divorce lawyer and the last time I'd seen him was on the inside front page of the *Sketch*, waltzing out of court with the Countess of Kinnoul or someone just after she'd been awarded two-hundred thou' and care of the cat. Anyhow, the one thing I knew for certain was that if Tommy wanted to see me there'd be money involved somewhere, and so, not more than twelve hours later, there I was at his offices, which were in one of those little squares somewhere between the Strand and the river, being waved into his room as if I were Edgar Wallace bringing his latest to the printer. It was only half-nine or so, but Tommy was already smoking a cigar a foot long and had all the society columns laid out on his desk, with half the paragraphs underlined in red ink.

'Research,' he explained, when I saw what he was doing. 'You'd be surprised how many times I get an instruction after someone drops a hint about hubby in the *Express*. How's tricks?'

So I told him about Abraxas, and Ma Fanshawe and lugging the Ceps kit up and down the Edgware Road, while Tommy listened with his head on one side and ran his finger over a letter he had rolled out on his knees. The suit he was wearing couldn't have cost less than thirty guineas, I reckoned.

'Odd kind of jobs you do,' he said when I'd finished. 'Now, how would you like it if I put you in the way of earning ten quid?'

'Wouldn't say no.'

'Thought not . . . Ever hear of a woman called Constantia Fenwick?'

Well, of course I'd heard of her. Who hadn't? You couldn't open a newspaper, especially one of the ones that went in for film gossip, without seeing a portrait of Constantia Fenwick. Mostly she played young ideal parts—you know, the girl who's living with her spinster aunt in the country and disgraces herself by falling for the gardener's boy, only he turns out to be a Cambridge undergrad down for the long vac and the heir to half a million.

'Wasn't she in *Daddy's Girl* with Victor Maclagan?'

'That's the one,' Tommy said. 'Well, Constantia —Miss Fenwick—is a client of mine. And the thing is, Montgomery hasn't been playing ball just lately.'

'Montgomery?'

'That's her husband.'

'I didn't know she was married.'

'Nobody does, much. They've managed to keep it out of the papers until now. Anyway, it's got to the point where he lies around the place all the time spending her money.'

Well, it sounded just the kind of life a chap could get used to, but I could see why Constantia Fenwick mightn't like it. Something struck me and I said:

'Is Constantia her real name?'

'Oddly enough, yes,' Tommy said. He was looking a bit irritated, so I decided to pipe down. 'Anyway, he tried to sell a story to the *Mail* last week all about how she was neglecting him and leaving their little girl to be brought up by the governess—you know the kind of thing. I got them to keep it out, but she says that's the last straw, and now she wants a divorce.'

'Where do I come in?'

Tommy's cigar had gone out, and he was relighting it with a sulphur match. As his sleeve flicked up there was a flash of diamond cuff-link. 'That's the interesting bit. Normally in these cases you offer the husband a settlement conditional on him pretending to be the guilty party.'

'Won't he do that?'

'No, he won't. Apparently he's a Baptist minister or something in his spare time. Says it would be against his principles. Plus there was a lot of stuff in that article about cinema being the Whore of Babylon, full of painted harlots. The long and short of it is that Constantia—Miss Fenwick—reckons that she's going to have to pretend to be the guilty party and get him to divorce her.'

'Will he do that?'

'He's a very religious man. Jealous, too. She says that if she's seen going down to Brighton for the night with another man, the papers'll be served within the week.'

'How will he find out?'

'Oh, we'll find ways of letting him know. You can be sure of that.'

'I still don't see where I come in.'

'Ah well, you're the chap who's going to go down to Brighton and pretend to be the co-respondent.'

I don't mind telling you this put me back a bit. I'd read bits in the paper about the fake co-respondent's lark, but I wasn't so sure what it would actually be like in practice. And what would Susie say if she got to hear about it, never mind the old lady? On the other hand, ten quid was ten quid,

114

and would solve most of my problems with Ma Fanshawe overnight. It might even buy me a week off work, and you can write a couple of decent-sized short stories in a week if you've a mind.

'It's the easiest thing in the world,' Tommy went on—he'd sensed my indecision, you see. 'Go down to Brighton on the train. Put up at the Grand—no expense spared, you know. Set your alarm for 6 a.m., toddle along the corridor to Constantia—Miss Fenwick's—suite and make sure the chambermaid finds you there when she brings in the breakfast. A kid could do it.'

'Won't her husband know it's a put-up job?'

'Like I said, he's a very religious man. It would be a matter of principle.'

'When would I have to go?'

'Tomorrow if you like. Twenty-four hours is all it would take. You could be back in London lunchtime the following day.'

That settled it. I'd been in on one or two of Tommy's schemes before, but there'd rarely been payment on delivery, so to speak. This way I'd have ten quid in my pocket the day after tomorrow. As for Constantia Fenwick, I was sure I could find enough to say to her to make the time pass pleasantly while we waited for the chambermaid to ferry in the kippers.

'I'll do it,' I said.

'Good man!' There was an effusiveness about Tommy as he said this that made me think I could have stood out for twenty, but it never does to overplay your hand. Five minutes later I was back in the Strand with one of Tommy's *Romeo y Julietas* as a souvenir and instructions to report to Victoria station at 2.30 p.m. the following afternoon. 'Any change of plan and I'll put you in the picture,' Tommy had said, 'but if I know Constantia—Miss Fenwick—she'll not hang about.'

It was one of those balmy mornings in early September, of the kind that Keats and co. used to get so dewy-eyed about. I walked down the Strand for a bit and into Fleet Street, watched a chap with a little nut-brown face and striped trousers, who could have been Beaverbrook himself, march into the *Express* building as if he owned it, and then went and had a cup of tea and a bun at a Lyons on the corner of Ludgate Circus—I'd had no breakfast, you see, what with Tommy's letter and the trek down from Paddington. All the time I was thinking about the ten quid and the new pair of shoes I was going to buy with it, not to mention the three quid that was booked for Ma Fanshawe. After that I sobered up a bit, went back to the office to collect the Ceps—Hastings winked at me from his doorway but he had the accountant with him going over the books—and then put in another eight hours in West Hampstead, which brought me all of fifteen bob. Part of me was wanting to go and meet Susie out of her office, but the other part was counselling caution. All that could wait, I reckoned, until I'd got back from Brighton and Tommy had his witness.

Anyhow, two-thirty the next afternoon found me parked under the clock at Victoria with a suitcase, watching a girls' school being packed onto a special, with half-a-dozen gym mistresses and what not barking orders at a volume that would have had a sergeant major sending out for earplugs. I couldn't have been there two minutes when a spindly looking bloke in a brown mac with a strand or two of silvery hair plastered across his head dawdled across from the newspaper kiosk and tapped me on the shoulder with a rolled-up copy of the *Mirror*.

'Your name Ross?'

'That's right.'

'I'm Mr Faulks. That the best suit you could find?'

'What's wrong with it?'

'Only joking, son. Brighton train's at platform ten. 'Ere's your ticket.'

The girls' school was still going by, and I could hear Daphne telling Virginia all about the ripping hols she'd had and how Evangeline was being made head monitor, but I took the hint and followed him over the asphalt to platform ten, wishing I had some extra fags for the journey. But he was a cheery chap for a private detective, and pretty soon we were hunched down in a second-class carriage under a picture of a woman in aviator goggles advertising Empire Tours and one of those posters telling you that Skegness was so bracing. A thought occurred to me, so I asked:

'Where's Miss Fenwick then?'

'Oh, she's coming down by a later train. They don't fraternize, y'know,' he went on, seeing the puzzled look on my face.

'So what's the form?'

'Lessee. It's jest gorn about three o'clock. Get to Brighton at four. You can hire a taxi to the Grand, or take the bus. It's up to you. Mr Kilmarnock won't mind either way. Then, once you've checked in, what you do in the next couple of hours is your own affair. Some of our people like to take a turn along the front. They do say the marina's worth a visit.'

There seemed to be something missing from this itinerary, so I said:

'When do I get to meet Miss Fenwick?'

'Lessee now, you ought to have dinner together. Right there in the middle of the restaurant so's everyone can see. And you definitely ought to walk up the staircase together afterwards. After that, well, Mr Kilmarnock'll have told you, breakfast's ordered for seven-thirty. All you have to do's be there in your dressing-gown.'

As a matter of fact, I hadn't got a dressing-gown, but I reckoned there was no need to let on to Faulks. I looked out of the window, where the south London suburbs—Clapham, Balham, Collier's Wood—were giving way to bits of countryside, scrubby-looking hedgerows, a distant view of the Downs. All this made me think of Netta, and a week we'd once spent in Sussex staying in a pub, and I suppose I must have gone a bit green about the gills as Faulks, who didn't seem a bad sort, split open a packet of Navy Cut, waved one in my face and said:

'Come on son, cheer up. Easiest ten quid anyone ever made. And you get to 'ave your dinner with Constantia Fenwick. How many blokes can say that?'

It was a fair point when you thought about it, so I took one of the fags, accepted a sandwich Faulks offered me out of a nest of greaseproof paper he had in his bag, and cheered up sufficiently to quiz him about his job, which wasn't a line of work I knew much about. He was a confiding soul, and by the time we got to Reigate I'd heard all about Lord Manningham having himself smuggled out of the back entrance of the Ritz to avoid the press

118

cameramen and the Marchioness of Wincanton putting ground glass in her husband's Brown Windsor soup to murder him. All this made the journey pass pleasantly enough, but by the time we got to Brighton I was down in the dumps again, with this queer sense of foreboding right down in the pit of my stomach. Worse, it had started to rain and there were puddles all over the station forecourt.

'Should get a taxi if I were you,' Faulks said. He looked horribly earnest and a bit excited, like a fox-hound catching the scent.

'Want a lift?'

'That would be collusion, wouldn't it?'

'Where do you get to stay?'

'That 'ud be telling,' Faulks said mysteriously. He took a black leather wallet out of his pocket, pulled out two ten-bob notes and pressed them into my hand.

'Expenses. But no overdoing it, mind. We had a chap once who went and blue'd the lot at the races.'

There was a bus stop on the other side of the road, and I watched him make his way slowly across, glaring furiously at the skidding cars. Then I hailed a cab and had myself taken off to the Grand. Do you know those Brighton hotels, I wonder? This one was the swankiest I'd ever been in, with tropical palms in outsize tubs all over the foyer and half-a-dozen women who could have come straight out of *Vogue* parked on the row of basket chairs. Still, Tommy had done his stuff and once I'd announced myself as Mr Ross the chap on the desk practically abased himself on the carpet before me, summoned a flunkey to carry my case and gave me a bow that wouldn't have disgraced a duke's butler, all the time shooting me glances that suggested my presence at the Grand was the best news the shareholders had had all year. Wanting to enter into the spirit of the thing, I put on my toniest accent, flicked an imaginary speck of dust off my cuff and enquired: had Miss Fenwick arrived yet? She hadn't, of course, but I received the news with a grave but gracious nod, whereupon the flunkey and I set off to my room—halfway along the third floor and with a view out over the front. When he'd put the bag down and made a pretence of straightening the bed sheets I tipped him two bob, ordered a double brandy to steady my nerves and sat down at a desk covered with expensive stationery to mull things over.

It was by now about half-past four, and the rain, which had been coming down pretty heavily while I was in the taxi, had eased off a bit. In the distance I could see the breakers coming in. The sea was an odd kind of blue-grey colour, a bit like the gravy Netta's mother used to serve up for Sunday lunch. They started serving dinner at the Grand at seven-thirty, so that left three hours to kill. For a moment I wondered about writing to the old lady on one of the hotel's embossed letter-heads, but I knew if I did she'd want to know why I was staying at the Grand in the first place. Then I wondered about ordering another double brandy, only something told me I ought to keep myself fresh for the evening. So in the end—the rain had pretty much stopped by now—I went for a walk along the front. Truth to tell, there wasn't a great deal to see. One or two of the newspaper bills said that Mr Lobby Ludd of the *News Chronicle* would be on the promenade that afternoon, but the trippers had all gone and I reckoned Mr Lobby Ludd, if he had any sense, would be soaking in the nearest pub or taking a squint at Miss Phyllis Dixey's *artistes*, who I'd noticed were on at one of the theatres.

So I mooched along for a bit, thinking that things weren't going too badly and staring into the shop windows every now and then: they go in for Kewpie dolls a lot in Brighton, and antimacassars—I can't think why. There was even a line for the poem I'd promised Susie stirring in my head—something about menacing winds—when all of a sudden a tallish chap with sandy-coloured hair and a big moustache breezed by on the other side of the road and I stopped and did a double-take. Either it was Rasmussen or he had a twin brother who'd decided to take himself down to Brighton for the day. By the time I'd taken a proper look at him he was a good ten yards away, so I turned on my heel and, trying not to make a great show of what I was about, followed him back up the road. He was going at no end of a lick—there was a little grey attaché case in his hand, bouncing against his hip as he went—but I'm no slouch myself, and by dint of keeping to the kerb and not being too particular about the people I bumped into I managed to keep him in my sights for the next 100 yards or so.

As I went I tried to work out whether it really was Rasmussen or simply someone who looked very like him, but no, I was sure it was him: he had a kind of dot-and-carry walk that I'd first noticed when I saw him sway along City Road, plus a habit of stopping every now and then and wiping his nose with the back of his hand. But what was he doing in Brighton, I wondered. Anyway, this went on for about twenty minutes—Rasmussen, or his double, pounding along the front, and then into some side streets full of genteel little shops, me following rapidly but discreetly in his wake. There was a moment, when he stood waiting by a pedestrian crossing, when I saw him in profile, but before I could get a decent look he was off again, and it was exactly the same walk as I'd seen in the character skipping down into the City Road basement with Susie sitting there in her A-line skirt obediently waiting to take dictation.

It was about half-five by now, most of the shops were shutting down, and half of me wondered whether I shouldn't be making tracks back to the Grand. Rasmussen, too, seemed to have doubts about the mission he was embarked on. Instead of blazing on into the sunset he kept on stopping to look into the shop-fronts. There was even a moment when he doubled back to stare at something he'd missed the first time around, and I thought it prudent to be tying up my shoelaces. This went on for nearly half-an-hour. I daresay a really top-class sleuth, a real Sexton Blake, would have got into conversation with him, found out where he was staying and picked his pocket into the bargain, but I don't have that kind of nerve. In any case I was already thinking about my date with Constantia Fenwick. Plus the rain looked as if it might be about to start up again and I knew the worst thing would be to get back to the hotel soaking wet, as there was nothing much to change into. So, with a last regretful look at Rasmussen, who was now taking an interest in the window of a bric-a-brac shop, I jumped into a cab that happened to be in sight and had myself taken back to the Grand.

Curiously enough, the first person I saw after I'd

paid off the cabbie was Faulks. He was standing on the front steps, as the porters surged around him and expensive-looking women and their attentive men folk sashayed by.

'Miss Fenwick here yet?' I asked.

'Turned up half-an-hour since. Suite on the third floor.'

'Shall I go up to her room and say hello?'

'Go up to her room?' Faulks looked genuinely put out. 'The idea! I should think not. No, you're to meet in the restaurant. There's a reservation for seven forty-five.'

'What's she like then, this Miss Fenwick?' I asked. The people were still streaming past us on either side, and a woman with a face like a Derby winner was asking someone called Hubert what he'd done with the travelling rugs.

'Miss Fenwick?' For the first time in our acquaintance he looked a bit sharp. 'Actress, isn't she?'

'Meaning?'

'No morals, have they?'

'Is that so?'

'Of course. Has to be. It's her husband I feel sorry for.'

'Why him in particular?'

'Don't suppose he has a square meal in a month. Never mind the carryings on. Did you see her in *Thanks a Million*?'

'I missed that one.'

'Wearing a two-piece bathing costume, she was. Indecent, I call it.' He was getting a bit worked up by now. You could imagine him out with the Watch Committee shining torches on the courting couples in the cinema back row. 'I'm not blaming *you*, mind.

123

No offence.'

'None taken.'

'If I were you I'd just go inside and enjoy myself.'

'That's right.'

It was starting to rain again, so I went inside to enjoy myself.

*   *   *

By the time I'd got back to my room (where the corners of the bed had been drawn back and there was a basket of fruit on the sideboard), given my suit a good going-over and inked in a couple of the holes I'd discovered in my socks, it was still only a quarter to seven. There was a Gideon's Bible in the drawer of the bedside table, but a couple of minutes with Sodom and Gomorrah, and Lot's wife soon quashed my interest in that, so I decided to head downstairs to the lounge bar and try and amuse myself there. Oddly enough, there was hardly anyone about except for an old boy in mustard-coloured plus-fours reading the *Morning Post*, but someone had left a copy of *Tatler* lying on a chair, and what with that and a brandy cocktail I ordered to keep me company, the time just raced away. I was getting used to the place now, which meant that I didn't leap up guiltily when the waiter went by, but sent him off to the bar to fetch another schooner of nuts. We know how to behave, you see, us Rosses, when push comes to shove. I had a friend once who used to hang around in hotel bars trying to get picked up by rich old women: he said you could make a decent living out of it, but the moult from the fox furs gave him asthma. Anyhow, come twenty to eight I'd had enough of reading about Lady Priscilla Piprag's *fête champêtre* at Puffbuttock Hall and, with a last look in the glass of one of those Guinness adverts that hung on the wall, I sailed off to the dining room in search of the evening's entertainment.

I didn't have very far to look. She was sitting at a table at the very centre of the room, with a couple of waiters soft-soaping her like Cleopatra's charioteers. My first thought was that she was a hell of a lot older than she seemed on the films: not so far off my age if it came to that. Quite a bit plumper, too. She saw me coming across the room—the waiters had faded away at my approach—and had a hand extended before I got there.

'You must be Mr Ross,' she said.

'That's me. How do you do?'

'I've been better, thanks.' And then I noticed something else, which was that the bottle of wine at her elbow, which couldn't have been open more than ten minutes, was already halfway down. As it happened, I'd spent a quarter of an hour or so in the lounge bar pondering some kind of conversational ice-breaker, and this seemed as good a time for it as any.

'Wonderful September weather we're having,' I said, as I slid into my chair.

'Christ,' Miss Fenwick said. She was smoking a cigarette out of an amber holder and looked as if she'd chew your head off for sixpence. 'I suppose we may as well eat, now that you're here. What'll you have?'

There was a menu card lying face down on the table, so I picked it up.

'I'm supposed to be watching my weight,' she said. 'But you can have what you like. Liberty Hall,

125

this is.'

And then I noticed another thing, which was that whereas on the screen she sounded like the Roedean elocution mistress, here behind a dinner table with half a bottle of wine inside her there was a distinct trace of Birmingham.

'I'll have the fish,' I said. There was a nice-looking baked turbot at eleven and sixpence.

'Fish it is. Have far to come?'

'Just London.'

'Dear old London, eh?' I thought this might be the prelude to some star-spangled bout of reminiscence, but no, all she did was to take another puff on the amber holder, make a bridge out of her folded hands and stare into space between them. The restaurant was filling up now, and there were at least half-a-dozen people craning their necks to get a proper look at her. The waiter who came to take our order fairly sprinted over from the banquette.

'Don't mind my asking,' I said—there was another bottle of wine on the table by this time, which I'd taken a glass of—'but what was it like working with Victor Maclagan?'

She gave me a look—disdainful, but kind of half-interested, too. 'Vic? He's all right. Perfect gentleman. Keeps himself to himself. I like that in a man. But you know who I couldn't stand?'

'No.'

'Kim Peacock.'

'What's the matter with him then?'

'Halitosis. Get within a foot of him and it's like a gust from the grave. I had to kiss him once. I was swilling mouthwash for the rest of the afternoon.'

Just then she had to go off and powder her nose.

126

A waiter came over carrying the fish and I caught his eye as he jerked the plate down.

'Busy this evening?'

'You can say that again.' Somehow he'd clocked me for a sympathizer. 'They're coming in here tonight like rats up a drainpipe.'

'Like a fag?'

'You're a toff.' He stuck the cigarette behind his ear. 'You take my tip, chum, and when it comes to the dessert give the peach melba a miss.'

'I'll do that. Thanks.'

Curiously enough, I was still thinking of my hike down the front in pursuit of Rasmussen—if it was him. Here in the Grand, with a comfortable chair under me and Lord and Lady Fortyskewer looking on from the next table, it seemed less likely. What was he doing in Brighton? While I thought about this I ate some of the fish, which wasn't at all bad, and watched Constantia come back from the ladies' room. She was a bit wobbly on her feet and did a circuit of the table before she sat down.

'Enjoying yourself?'

'Top-hole thanks.'

'They give you a decent room?'

'Can't complain.'

A man in a dinner jacket and dicky bow who'd been hovering around us for the past minute or two now bent his bald head over the table.

'Do I have the honour of addressing Miss Fenwick?'

'That's me.'

'It would give me the greatest satisfaction to possess your signature, Miss Fenwick.'

'Bloody cheek,' she said, speaking the words to me, rather than to him. 'How would he like it if I came up to him while he was eating his dinner and asked for his autograph? Waiter!'

The bloke I'd given the fag to was at her elbow in a tick.

'Yes, madam.'

'Would you kindly tell this gentleman to go away?'

'Would you go away please, sir, and stop annoying the lady?'

The man in the dinner jacket slunk spiritlessly away. 'Bloody cheek,' she said again. 'How was the fish?'

'A1.'

'Do you know, I feel unaccountably hungry. Haven't had a bite since yesterday afternoon, not since I started to bant. Waiter!'

'Yes, madam.'

'Bring me a peach melba, would you? There's a good chap.'

I didn't have the heart to say anything. While we were waiting she looked round the room once or twice very curiously, as if she couldn't work out who the people were or why they'd come there. Then she picked up a fork, stared at it very hard and held it out over the dining table as if it was a divining-rod.

'Do you know?' she said. 'I've got a good mind to give all this up.'

We were well into the third bottle of wine by now. 'Give what up?'

'All this. The films and everything. Going to the Embassy every other Friday night, because if I don't the man from the *Sketch*'ll wonder why I'm not there. Do you know what I'd really like to do?'

'No.'

'I'd like to open a tea shop. One of those classy ones. You know. Where they serve Fuller's walnut cake and seven different kinds of tea. With the waitresses got up like parlour-maids. Not like a Lyons. I hate those Lyonses.'

The peach melba came then, and she ate some of it, still telling me about the classy tea shop she fancied running. Then she said: 'You'll have to excuse me a moment.'

She was gone a very long time.

*   *   *

Somehow I managed to set the alarm clock I'd brought with me for 6 a.m., but as it turned out I needn't have bothered. After what seemed about ten minutes since I'd gone to sleep I felt myself being shaken awake by someone waving an electric lamp in my face.

'F——!'

'Steady, steady,' said the bloke who was doing the shaking. It was Mr Faulks. Here in the haggard early light—it was just before dawn—he looked quite deathly, as if he'd just been dug up and come back to haunt me. For all that, he seemed amused about something.

'What the f—— are you doing?' I bawled. As well as the shock, my head felt as if someone had just driven a coach and horses through it.

'Hold on now,' Mr Faulks said. 'No need to get excited.' He had what looked like a telegram in his hand. 'Come to think of it, there's no need to get out of bed at all.'

'Why's that?' I was sitting up against the pillows now, and reaching for the glass of water I'd left on the bedside table.

'It's all off. Mr Kilmarnock's orders. Seems her 'usband's found out.'

I couldn't understand this at all. 'Isn't that a good thing?'

'I can see you're new to this game,' said Mr Faulks, with a sniff. 'Last thing we want is a scene. Prejudices everybody—judge, newspapers, the lot. Having him finding her here is bad enough. No, you'd best be on your way. Have another hour's kip if you like, but after that I'd take it kindly if you'd make yourself scarce. And don't you go down to the breakfast room, neither.'

'So that's it, is it?' I was thinking about my ten quid.

'Looks like it. For the moment, anyway.'

'But why?'

'Like I said, can't have you hanging about here when her husband turns up.'

'Why not?'

'He's a very religious man. There's no telling what he might do. I was on a case once,' said Mr Faulks—his little black eyes were darting excitedly in his chalk-white face—'when a chap found his wife having breakfast in her room—you know, just like you were planning to do—a kipper apiece and scrambled eggs waiting—and he pinned the other chap's hand to the bedhead with a fork.'

* * *

What do you do in such circumstances? Come eight o'clock I was standing outside the Grand waiting for a taxi to take me back to the station. Faulks, who even in extremity was a good sort, had said he'd sub me breakfast, but apparently the expenses had already been on the high side and it turned out that all he could manage was a bob, which paid for a bacon sandwich and a cup of tea at the station caff, plus ten Park Drive, as between you and me my nerves weren't in tip-top condition. I hadn't liked to ask about the ten quid, as I knew pretty well what the answer would be. It was one of those grey mornings you get by the coast in September, with the wind coming in off the sea, the gulls parked on the telephone wires and the breeze stirring up the ice-cream wrappers in the doorways, and I sat in the caff browsing through a copy of that morning's *Argus*, which was on about razor-gangs at the horse races and a burglary someone had done in a jeweller's shop that night. My head still felt as if I'd been trampled on by half-a-dozen prize heifers, but funnily enough I'd cheered up a bit. In fact, there were two things I was pretty confident about. One was getting a quid or two out of Tommy in compensation for lost wages. The other was that Susie and I were going to have that weekend in the country if I had to do a year's overtime to pay for it.

10 FRIENDS AND RELATIONS

Sound Advice for the Salesman: VI. Fortitude

The best salesman adopts a realistic attitude towards his work. There will be days when even the most successful operator 'does not feel up to it' or 'would rather be somewhere else', when the thought of another street to be canvassed or the face of another customer staring from her doorway is simple torture. Remember! It is in adversity that the champion salesman flourishes. It is when the salesman has his back to the wall that his eyes should be at their keenest. The successful salesman is not deterred by down-heartedness, bad weather or discouragement— all the things that the feeble individual uses as an excuse. No! He makes a virtue of his setbacks by using them as a spur to the achievement of yet greater heights. Ask him how he has succeeded and he will tell you—through tenacity, the 'bulldog spirit', grit, pluck, verve, an inner resolution, the voice ringing in his ear that assures him: 'Never give up 'til the sale is won!'

Abraxas Salesman's Handbook

'All right now,' the little man said. He was breathing heavily and there were beads of sweat standing out on his pale, knobby forehead. 'Repeat after me.' He began to recite in a high, sing-song voice: *'I am here to make the sale. The sale is here to be made. My destiny is to make the sale.'*

Fact is, I've got no self-consciousness at times like this, and I bawled it out happily enough. It was a bit like being in church back at Tenterden, with the old lady mumbling into her prayer book and the sidesman looking down his nose at the sixpence I'd put in the collection plate. But the two chaps squeezed into the desk in front of me—who'd been sniggering to each other while the little man worked himself up into a lather—could barely raise a cheep.

'Here now,' the little man said. He was a tiny bloke, not much above five feet high, with sandy hair and one of those toothbrush moustaches that the subalterns used to wear in the war. 'Here now. That won't do at all, that won't. Think you're going to sell anything with an attitude like that? No, my friends, what you need is gumption. G-U-M-P-T-I-O-N. Now, repeat after me,' his Adam's apple was going up and down like a tomahawk—'*I am the sale. The sale is here to be made. My destiny is to make the sale.*'

'*I am here to make the sale,*' I yelled out, not caring how goofy I sounded. '*The sale is here to be made. My destiny is to make the sale.*'

It was about half-past twelve on a Thursday morning, a week after the Brighton fiasco, and we were down in the basement at Doughty Street. Outside, the autumn was finally in prospect and there were rust-coloured leaves all over the pavements and strips of torn newspaper blowing around the gutters. The pep-up sessions, as they were known, were Roper's idea (he was getting better now, Hastings said, and no longer thought there were spiders crawling out of the lino) and took place twice a week. They were mostly taken by the little man with the toothbrush moustache but once there'd been a lugubrious old buffer in spongebag trousers who had us sing what sounded like a revivalist hymn with a chorus that went '*I'm going to get that foot of mine right in the door, right in the door.*' I daresay this sounds ludicrous to you, but I've known worse. There was a vacuum cleaner outfit in Bognor who'd made its reps file up and down a church hall with placards while the sales manager harangued them from a lectern.

'Christ!' one of the blokes in front of me said, *sotto voce*, to the other, 'this 'ere's like the f——g Salvation Army.'

There were about a dozen of us there: recent recruits, mostly, who I hardly recognized. One or two of them looked as if they'd only just left school. Hastings sat on his own by the door, pulling on a Gold Flake. He looked especially bored.

'That was much better,' the little man with the toothbrush moustache said. He was still breathing hard. '*Much* better.'

For some reason the sight of him, keen as mustard and clearly getting no end of a kick, reminded me of all the jobs I'd had. There'd been plenty of them all right. Clerk in an office in the City. Photographer's assistant. Lifeguard at the Brixton lido. Even teaching fretwork in a boys' school once. 'Never could stick to anything,' the old lady used to say, and she was bang right. It was the same now. What with the autumn coming and the leaves falling over the heaths, like the ones that strewed the brooks in Vallombrosa, wherever that was, I'd much rather have been out somewhere with Susie: Richmond Park, say, or out on the towpath at Staines, where you can walk for miles and not see

134

more than a couple of old women with their dogs or one of those bottle-nosed old Thames fishermen.

The meeting was breaking up now. The two blokes who'd been sitting in front of me were having a conversation about the four-thirty at Market Rasen and how Star of David might be expected to do over the jumps, and the little man with the toothbrush moustache was sitting back in his chair, completely blown, wolfing a bar of Caley's marching chocolate. I was just about to head for the staircase when Hastings reached out and tweaked my arm.

'Going back out on the rounds?'

'That's the idea.' I'd got three quid put by now, but the weekend at Newcome Grange wasn't near enough paid for, and Tommy, despite lending a sympathetic ear over the Brighton business, had only come up with thirty bob for what he called the 'inconvenience'.

'Well, come and have a drink first. My shout.'

'Don't mind if I do.'

Between you and me I did mind. I was spending a lot of time in the pub with Hastings these days. He was one of those blokes who don't seem to function properly unless they're in sight of a barmaid and a double row of pint glasses. We went to a little place round the corner in Roger Street, which was usually full of lawyers' clerks talking about peppercorns and fee simples.

'Queerest thing in the world about that chap Callender,' he said, when we were sitting at one of the little wooden tables with a pint of mild and bitter apiece. 'You could have knocked me down with a feather when I heard.'

'What exactly were they after him for?' I asked.

135

It was the first time we'd talked about Callender's arrest.

'Something down on the south coast,' Hastings said. There was a Sally Ann girl by the bar selling copies of the *War Cry* and he bought one and rolled it out on the table between us. 'Been after him for ages, apparently.'

'You know it was coming?'

'Can't say I did.'

'When I first knew him,' I said, 'down in Bognor, it was always supervisors' wives.'

'Looks as if I had a lucky escape then,' Hastings said. I couldn't tell if he was joking or not.

The headline in the *War Cry* was something about calling sinners to repent before it was too late. Hastings stared at it while he took another pull at his pint. He seemed even more depressed than when we'd been watching the little bloke with the toothbrush moustache yelling at us about motivation.

'Here,' he said. 'What do you make of this religion business?'

You got this quite a lot on the door-to-door, but it was the first time anyone I worked for had asked me.

'What? God and the Bible and so on?'

'That's right. Do you believe in God?'

'Oh I believe in him all right. But I don't think he likes me very much.'

'You don't, eh?'

'No.'

One of the lawyers' clerks had heard the end of this exchange and was looking at me as if I was a baboon that'd just escaped from the zoological gardens, but it was all the same to me.

136

'Did you know,' Hastings said, not waiting for a reply and still staring at the stuff about sinners repenting before it was too late, 'that my wife used to be a Jehovah's Witness? Very devout girl she was. Strictly brought up, too. When we were courting it was all I could get her to do to hold my hand. Of course, I respected that in her. And then, after we'd been married a year or so she gave it all up.'

'Why was that?'

'Well, she said it was because someone had told her the world was going to end on 13 June 1921. And then, when it didn't, she said she'd look silly if she went any more.'

'But what about the others? Wouldn't they have looked silly as well?'

'That's what I said.' I'd seen a photo of Mrs Hastings, who, contrary to all expectations, was a bit of a looker. 'You want the other half of this?'

'I ought to get back to Somers Town.'

'That's the spirit.'

'That reminds me,' I said. 'I shan't be in next Friday. Nor the Saturday morning either. Going away for the weekend.'

'With your girl, eh?'

'In a manner of speaking.'

'I never had any luck with women,' Hastings said. 'That's not to say anything against my wife, you understand. But if I told you some of the things that had happened to me in that line, I daresay you'd be astonished.'

It was no good. I knew if I stayed listening to Hastings talk about women I'd be there until closing time, so I hoisted up the Ceps kit, which I'd taken the precaution of bringing with me from the

137

office, and made my excuses.

'Hang on,' Hastings said. 'Something else I was meaning to ask you. Those pep-up sessions. Do you think they do any good?'

'Bound to,' I said. 'Just the sort of thing you need sometimes to buck you up a bit.'

'Do you really think so?' Hastings said. 'That's what Roper says, but I've always had my doubts you know.'

Outside in Doughty Street I propped the Ceps kit up against a plane tree, fished in my pocket for a fag and smoked it looking through some iron railings into a basement where three or four girls in hair-nets sat packing what looked like bits of ladies' underwear into cardboard boxes. You got some odd businesses in Doughty Street. Fact is, what with Susie and Haversham and the weekend at Newcome Grange, my nerves were shot to pieces. For two pins I'd have lugged the Ceps kit back to the office and spent the afternoon boozing with Hastings, but I knew I'd kick myself if I didn't get back on the road. And all the time, too, I was worrying about the fix I'd be getting myself into. Surely you could get arrested for turning up under false pretences at someone's country house for the weekend? What would Susie say if that happened? In the end, though, I calmed down. I knew that if I didn't do it Haversham could have all kinds of fun at my expense. Plus it was a heaven-sent opportunity to spend a couple of days in the same house as Susie. Two days with Susie! Who knew what might happen? And so I sat on the bus as it chugged up Theobald's Road, with my feet wound around the Ceps kit to stop it sliding down the gangway and my eyes fixed on the poster saying

Skegness was so bracing, thinking about the weekend, while the wind blew more leaves out over the pavement and the sky threatened rain.

As I might have expected, the afternoon was a frost. Nobody was in, or if they were in they weren't buying. The closest I got to a sale was with a blonde woman with a squint in her eye who was on the point of going off for her purse when her husband came home unexpectedly and more or less kicked me out into the street. Worse, about half-past three it began to rain, and I'd done something to my arm, what with lugging the Ceps kit about, that made it hurt like hell.

Anyway, standing on the doorstep of the chap who'd chucked me out, I had a bright idea. I'd stash the kit back at the office and then go over to City Road, where there was a fair chance that Rasmussen might not be in and I could hang around and talk to Susie. Come four o'clock— it was raining like anything and I was glad I had my mac on—I was heading off east towards the City. By now it had turned into one of those foul September afternoons where the buses sweep up sheets of water over the pavements and you can feel the rain soaking through your trouser-bottoms, but I didn't mind. There were paper-sellers out hawking the early evening editions—all about the financial crisis, as usual, and what Ramsay Mac had said at the Lord Mayor's dinner—but at this moment in time I couldn't have cared less if the whole Stock Exchange had slid off its moorings into the Thames.

Funny how you get premonitions about things. When I got the letter from Netta telling me it was all U-P, I'd known for hours it would be coming.

Somehow I had a feeling there wouldn't be anyone in Rasmussen's office, and so it turned out. The electric light was on and someone had left a parcel propped up against the door, but though I knocked a couple of times no one came. I was just wondering whether to head for the Lyons over the way when a burly kid in a blue suit that was too tight for him came crashing down the steps so fast that he had to fling out both arms to stop himself going head-first through the plate glass. When he saw me, he said:

'I thought you was f——g Rasmussen.'

'Well I'm not, am I?'

He gave me another look, not exactly hostile but not gleaming with brotherly love either.

'F——g good job you aren't.'

'Is that so?'

He was a big lad, about nineteen or twenty, six foot tall and built like something out of the London Irish back row, with the vilest cockney accent I'd heard since the week I put in pushing trolleys at Billingsgate. Anyhow, when he saw I was harmless he turned a bit more conciliatory, tried to light a fag and swore disgustedly when the match went out.

'Been hanging round 'ere [*rahned eayer*] all f——g afternoon, f—— it.' He'd got the fag going by now. 'What you 'ere to see old Rasmussen about?'

'Not him I'm here for.'

'No?' Must be the secretary [*sekerterry*] then. Well, there's a fair few on that game.' He was holding the fag daintily between finger and thumb, I noticed, rather like the old lady on the three occasions a year when someone persuaded her to smoke. 'No offence or anything.'

'None taken.'

Somewhere in the distance a clock was striking the half. In another hour it'd be dark. The kid stood listening to the chimes and then shook his head.

'Can't hang about here [*ang abaht year*],' he said. 'Got a feller to see in Canning Town. You see Rasmussen, you tell him I was here, OK?'

'I'll do that.'

'You're a f——g toff.'

'That's what people say.'

I watched his feet disappearing up the steps with the vaguely interested feeling you get when there's trouble in store for someone but mercifully the lucky chap isn't you, but wondering who the fair few ones on that game might be. The rain was coming down even harder now, and I was just wondering whether to sling my hook altogether when there was another patter of feet and Susie came tripping into view.

'Gracious,' she said. 'What are you doing here?'

'I was just passing,' I told her. She was wearing one of those shiny red mackintoshes with a kind of hood that was drawn tight over her hair. 'You just missed a visitor. Tough-looking chap. None too choice with his language.'

'That must be Leo. He's always hanging round here. Did he say what he wanted?'

'Just that he needed to see Mr Rasmussen.'

'He's always hanging round here,' she said again, sounding slightly annoyed.

'He looked a bit of a tough customer to me.'

'I suppose he is, rather.'

She had the door unlocked by this time and was standing in the vestibule taking off her mac. 'Oh dear,' she said.

'What's the matter?'

'Well, if it had been yesterday or the day before I could have made you a cup of tea. But Mr Rasmussen will be back any moment. He's gone to buy himself a new evening suit. He says his old one won't do for Newcome Grange.' For a moment I wondered whether to spill the beans about Jimmy's invitation, but then I thought it would be more sensible to keep my mouth shut. 'Did you know,' she said, 'that Mrs Reginald Heber and Mr Burnage are coming?'

Burnage was a comedian I'd once seen on a variety bill with Harry Tate.

'Who's Mrs Reginald Heber?'

'I don't know. You see her name in the papers a lot . . . Look, you must go. Here!'

And then I was kissing her as if there were no tomorrow, with one hand grasping the back of her neck and my eyes full of red hair, and a postman whistling with glee as he came marching down the steps with a fistful of letters in his hand to surprise us. It was like Piccadilly Circus that afternoon. After that I bounced back along the City Road as if the pavement was made of India rubber, but also thinking that there was something odd about Mr Rasmussen and his basement, what with East End hooligans dropping in for a chat and a couple of dozen watches laid out over the boss's desk—that had been the view from over Susie's shoulders, whenever I got the hair out of my eyes. No point in pretending that it wasn't any of my business either, given how thick I was with Haversham and the people at West End Central.

I was still thinking about Mr Rasmussen's basement, and the pile of watches, and Susie—

142

mostly about Susie—when I turned into Sispara Gardens around quarter-past five. It had that usual flyblown, late-afternoon look—a kid or two delivering papers in the gathering gloom, a middle-aged bloke in shirt sleeves trying to crank up a car, a Jack Russell doing its business on the kerb—but I could see as I came along that there was a chap in an overcoat and a bowler hat hanging around outside Ma Fanshawe's gate. For a moment I assumed it was Haversham, until a glance at the way the chap was lounging by the gate and the tilt of his bowler hat told me that it was someone a lot more familiar. In fact it was my Uncle George.

'I asked inside,' he said, a bit diffidently, when I got within earshot, 'and they said you'd be back soon.'

'What do you want?'

I don't think I've told you about my Uncle George. He was a tall, thin character of about sixty, not bad looking in a way, and the old lady's younger brother, which meant that he belonged to the no-hope plebeian side of the family. At one point just after the war he'd had some kind of job in theatrical management, but since then he'd drifted around the place selling advertising on commission. He was supposed to be married, but no one—not even the old lady—had ever met his wife. I hadn't seen him for upwards of eighteen months.

'That's no way to greet your old uncle,' he said, a bit indignantly, as I slid the catch on the gate and stepped inside. 'Half an hour I've been waiting here. Rained too, and me without an umbrella.'

'You'd better come in and have a cup of tea,' I said. A courteous nephew who meant well by him would have taken him off to the pub, but I wasn't

143

a courteous nephew. Besides, I had two quid in my pocket, and Uncle George drank like a champion.

Still, he was my uncle, and as we plodded up Ma Fanshawe's staircase, where some plutocrat had left two or three empty fag packets jammed up against one of the rails just to make the rest of us envious, I took a proper look at him. For a man who stuck to an exclusive diet of Charringtons and Player's Navy Cut he looked in pretty good shape. Jaunty, too, which always made me suspicious. Us Rosses are regular doom and gloom merchants, you understand.

'What brings you to London?' I asked as we came into my room, which thankfully wasn't quite as debauched-looking as it might have been.

'Oh, business you know. And Elsie'—Elsie was his wife—'wanted to see the sights. Cigarette?'

Uncle George had an infallible trick when it came to offering people fags. This was to keep a packet of Weights in his breast pocket with a single cigarette mouldering inside the flap. On opening the packet he would then say: 'Damn! I could have sworn I had a full packet.' Nine out of ten people would then offer him one of their own instead. But I was the tenth person and I was wise to Uncle George.

'Thanks very much.'

It was an ancient cigarette that had lain long in the packet—quite possibly the original cigarette that had begun his career as a fag-scrounger—and while I smoked it and made the tea Uncle George silently agonized over its loss, settled himself in one of the chairs and cast a quick eye over the room.

'With your education you could do better than

this,' he said.

'I do all right.'

'That's not what your mother says.'

As the old lady cordially detested Uncle George and wouldn't let him in the house, I couldn't see how he'd come by this information.

'And that girl you were going to marry. Etta. What happened to her, eh?'

'Netta. We just decided we weren't cut out for each other.'

'It's a great mistake to get set in your ways,' Uncle George remarked sententiously. 'Worst thing you can do. That's my advice. Worst thing you can do. Why, if I hadn't married Elsie—and I was determined to do it, you know, despite her father taking against me—well, I don't know how my life would have turned out.'

I nearly yelled: *so how did your life turn out then?* But that wasn't the way to handle Uncle George. You had to let him prose on a bit, with minimal interruption, until he got round to telling you what he wanted.

And so we sat there, with the rain dripping on the trees beyond the window and the sound of Ma Fanshawe's radio carrying up from the floor below and the occasional noise of one of the other lodger's boots on the stair, while Uncle George droned on about the newspaper advertising business and thirty quid that someone was supposed to have swindled him out of and the three-bedroom house he and Elsie inhabited in Ramsgate and his bronchitis, which was aggravating, and I thought about Susie some more, and the poem I was writing for her, which was about three-quarters done now, and the weekend at Newcome Grange that I still

145

hadn't properly worked out.

'You know,' Uncle George said—after about halfan-hour of this, when three tea cups lay empty on the tray before him—'your mother often says she wishes you'd go and live with her again.'

It seemed deuced unlikely to me, but I nodded. 'Does she?'

'That's right. Find your feet, she says.'

He was getting to his own feet now. Here in the artificial light he looked older, I saw. What had once been brindled hair was turning a badgerish silver. A big dollop of egg had fallen down the front of his Toc-H tie and left a stain. 'Good lord,' he exclaimed. He had his notecase out and was staring at it with an expression of mock incredulity that wouldn't have fooled a four-year-old.

'What's the matter?' I asked.

'Do you know,' he said, 'I must have forgotten to go to the bank this morning? Went clean out of my head for some reason. What with all the trouble of getting down here. And there's Elsie waiting at Charing Cross for me to take her home.'

'Won't Elsie have any money?' I suggested brightly.

But Uncle George was too practised a campaigner for this. 'Not if I know Elsie. She'll have spent it all on her tea, if I know Elsie.'

What do you do in such circumstances? I gave him a quid, which he pocketed with one of those careless you-be-damned airs that would have done credit to George Robey, and stood watching as he shuffled down the stairs. About halfway down, when he thought I'd gone back inside, he stopped and picked up one of the empty fag packets just to see if there was anything left inside. Meanwhile

I was kicking myself. A whole quid to scrounging Uncle George! That left just under a pound for what I'd need towards Newcome Grange. Something told me that next morning I'd be getting up with the sparrows.

11

PIMLICO TO HIGHBURY

Mrs Eulalie Delisle's evening party, which I had the pleasure of attending yesterday, was the very height of Mayfair ton. The Hon. Mrs Pelly looked charming in pink, and I enjoyed a lively conversation with Miss Eleanor Whittlesea, the accomplished daughter of Sir Humphrey Whittlesea Bt., about a forthcoming foreign trip in celebration of her engagement to Captain Henry Chevenix: 'The banns will be said in Cannes,' as she amusingly put it. Others present included Lady Dashwood, the Hon. Myfanwy Pringle and Mr Edward Rasmussen . . .

'Mr Gossip' Daily Sketch, *7 September 1931*

Mr Rasmussen lived in a mews flat in Pimlico—not, as he was occasionally heard to say, quite what he had in mind, nor even especially convenient for his place of work, but fulfilling one of his great criteria for life, which was privacy. Quite what Mr Rasmussen did have in mind was difficult to say, for he was a secretive man, and none of the friends he had made in London had ever been invited to the

Pimlico mews: when Mr Rasmussen entertained he did so in the private rooms of West End hotels or supper clubs, and he paid for these entertainments in cash, leaving no trace of himself behind. Mr Rasmussen was thought to be Danish, and perhaps in the end the flat had a Baltic air. There were little jars of pickled herring on the shelves of the maplewood kitchenette, a bottle or two of cherry brandy on the sideboard and a watercolour of the Copenhagen Sound on the sitting-room wall. His habits were monastic. The light in the mews flat was always extinguished by ten o'clock at night, and he was generally out of the place by eight in the morning. Occasionally a little light classical music could be heard trickling down the staircase.

Most Saturday mornings, Mr Rasmussen could be found at one or other of his offices. On this particular Saturday morning—it was a fine day in early September—he was still sitting in one of the light, tubular chairs—Mr Rasmussen was horribly modernist in his tastes—that lay around his sitting room, drinking a very pungent cup of coffee and occasionally getting up from the chair to walk to the room's farther side. Here, squeezed in between a gramophone playing selections from Grieg and a drinks cabinet, stood a squat, gunmetal safe with a combination lock, empty of possessions and with its door half-open. Reaching the safe, in the course of these excursions from his chair, Mr Rasmussen performed a variety of manoeuvres. Sometimes he pushed the door to and then fiddled with the lock to make it open. Sometimes he took a small torch, no bigger than a pencil, out of his pocket and shone it into the lock's interior. Twice or thrice he rapped on the safe's metal exterior. Once he took the cup he had been drinking from and placed it inside the safe, locked the door and then twisted furiously to see if he could release it. Finding that he could, he turned his back on the safe, drank the remainder of the coffee and went back to his seat.

It was by now about eleven o'clock. Throughout his experiments with the safe, Mr Rasmussen had been dressed in his shirt-sleeves and an old pair of trousers. Now, picking up various items of post from the mat as he went, he proceeded to his bedroom. However sparsely furnished his living quarters, there was one thing Mr Rasmussen did possess in abundance, and that was suits. There were at least a dozen of them hanging in the wardrobe and he spent five minutes brooding over them before selecting one in light tweed, which might have suggested to anyone who saw him that its owner, though temporarily detained in London, had the prospect of a country weekend before him. Having donned the suit, polished his shoes with a rag, trimmed the ends of his moustache with the aid of a pair of scissors and a pocket mirror and thrown a last, lingering look at the safe, Mr Rasmussen picked up his hat, shut the door of the flat behind him, inspected the staircase beneath him, which was empty, and set off down the stairs.

It would be tedious to recount everything Mr Rasmussen did with his time over the next half-hour, but he certainly bought a newspaper and glanced at it as he walked in a leisurely way past Victoria station—an ant-heap in the Saturday morning rush, with taxis sailing in from all sides and buses jamming-up the approach roads—and into Belgravia. Here there was a street composed entirely of antique shops, and Mr Rasmussen looked through their windows in a very knowing way, once or twice producing a notebook from his inner pocket and jotting down details that occurred to him. There was a competition, currently advertised in one of the newspapers, in which competitors were invited to speculate upon a person's identity and professional calling from his appearance, but such people would have been flummoxed by Mr Rasmussen. He looked merely like a prosperous and well-dressed man strolling through Belgravia in the general direction of Knightsbridge, with a newspaper under his arm, bound no doubt for one of the big houses at its further end and a Saturday luncheon.

Reaching Lowndes Square, and looking, despite his half-hour's walk, as if he had just alighted from a taxi, Mr Rasmussen walked across to the eastern side, rapped on the door of Plantagenet House, surrendered his hat to the butler, wiped his feet superfluously on the mat and was shown up to the drawing room. There were only a dozen people there, for it was early September and most of London was out of town, but Mr Rasmussen smiled at them and seemed to know them. Anyone who listened to him as he went about these conversations, shook hands and bent to receive confidences, would not have said that he was memorable or even witty, but he was certainly very polite. When anyone asked him what his plans were for the weekend, he remarked that there was a stretch of the Solent that he hoped very much would have a salmon or two left in it for him.

Coming upon his hostess, framed by the bank of glass and mirrors, he said very mildly, 'Why Bertha, how are you, and how was Biarritz?' and

150

Mrs Antrobus said that she was very well and that Biarritz was tolerable. At luncheon, taken downstairs in the great dining room, he was placed between a deaf old lady, one of Mrs Antrobus's neighbours in the square, and an obscure MP who had not managed to get himself asked anywhere in Scotland, and exerted himself to be agreeable. Afterwards, over coffee, he had another fleeting conversation with his hostess. Was she still having trouble with that necklace, he wondered? And Mrs Antrobus said yes, it was still with the people in Cornhill as he had recommended. Whereupon Mr Rasmussen, changing the subject in the most natural way, said that he gathered Biarritz was getting very crowded these days and had she thought of Cannes?

The party broke up at three o'clock. Walking through the streets beyond Lowndes Square, Mr Rasmussen did not have the look of a man who hopes that the Solent has a salmon or two left in it for him. Outside the park gates he hailed a taxi and had himself borne away not to a railway terminus or to his flat, but to the eastern end of Oxford Street. The taxi having deposited him on the pavement outside Bourne & Hollingsworth, Mr Rasmussen stopped for a moment or two to get his bearings, looked at his watch, gave threepence to an accordion player with one eye and a row of medals, and plunged off southwards in the direction of Wardour Street. Here, turning right and left through a brace of alleyways, he arrived at a door set two or three feet into a grey-brick vestibule littered with cabbage stalks and bits of packing cases, on which someone had stencilled the words PEGASUS CLUB.

Mr Rasmussen seemed to know all about the Pegasus Club. He had himself admitted by a languid negro in an evening suit, and proceeded up a flight of wooden stairs towards a room where gramophone music was playing and one or two voices could be heard quietly conversing. As in the drawing room at Lowndes Square, Mr Rasmussen seemed perfectly at his ease. He ordered a glass of gin and angostura bitters, chatted affably to the young woman at the bar, who seemed to know him, nodded to one or two of the people around him and took his drink to a table at the very back of the club, where a surrealist painting hung on the wall, together with a notice requesting patrons not to compile betting slips.

Here Mr Rasmussen seemed perfectly content. He smoked a cigarette, which he took from a case in the pocket of his suit, a case so thinly wrought that it seemed not to spoil the garment's line, and spent twenty minutes over his gin and angostura bitters. His arrival had coincided with a curious depopulation of the club. When he looked up from his table at the end of his twenty minutes there was no one there but himself. Taking the empty glass back to the bar—the gramophone had stopped and the only sound was the noise of the negro whistling as he swept the stairs twelve feet below—he enquired of the barmaid: had she seen Davenport, or perhaps Hines? By way of an answer, the barmaid flicked her head in the direction of a small, interior room with a curtain of fringed beads hung across its entrance that lay to the right of the bar, and on her own initiative—for Mr Rasmussen had given no instruction—set three tumblers on a tray and poured double measures of whisky into them.

152

Mr Rasmussen meekly accepted the tray and took it through the bead curtain into the smaller room, where there were a couple of tables and a fruit machine into which a man of about twenty-two, with very short hair and a suit somewhere between mauve and purple, was feeding pennies, while another man, of about the same age but less picturesquely dressed, sat watching him. Seeing Mr Rasmussen, the short-haired man drew his hand away from the fruit machine, gave its frontage a despairing tap with his finger, accepted one of the three glasses of whisky, and said:

'F——g thing's fixed. Two bob and a tanner I've put in there, and not so much as a penny back.'

'Dear, dear,' said Mr Rasmussen. 'Well, well.' He found a penny in his pocket and pushed it into the slot of the machine, tugged the handle, watched the cylinders settle in the window and received threepence for his trouble.

'Where've you been then?' the second of the two men enquired, noting Mr Rasmussen's tweed suit. 'All dressed up like a pox-doctor's clerk.'

Mr Rasmussen laughed again, and drank a sip of his whisky. 'Dear me,' he said. 'Whatever do they put in this?'

'It's that yid stuff from Hoxton. They put raw spirit in it. What game you on then?'

The man who had brooded over the machine was called Davenport, and his companion Hines, and together they seemed to know a great deal about Mr Rasmussen. They asked him: had he been to the Vauxhall Road Empire recently, and were there any nice girls he could introduce them to, although 'nice girls' were not exactly the words used, and had he seen that Leo of late and given him any

153

more jobs to do? Mr Rasmussen bore all this with great affability, ordered cigars from the bar—the cigars were a great deal better than the whisky—and liberally distributed them. Then he said, quite easily:

'I think we may as well meet this evening, as arranged.'

'Place is the same?' Davenport asked.

'Well, Finsbury Square perhaps. Near the theatre.'

The gramophone had started up again in the main room, rather louder than before, and whatever else Mr Rasmussen may have said was obscured by the sound of Nellie Wallace.

My mother said
'Always look under the bed.
Before you blow the candle out,
Make sure there's no man about.'
Da da-da da da . . .

Presently Mr Rasmussen took his leave. There was a clock striking four as he came out into Wardour Street, and men selling early editions of the evening newspapers. On the corner of Wardour Street and Shaftesbury Avenue he hailed another taxi and had himself carried off through the Saturday crowds to a remote and desolate part of Islington. Set down on a street corner next to one or two melancholy shops, he walked for a little way into a region of courtyards and lock-up garages, produced a key from his waistcoat pocket and let himself into a little brick shed with a battered tin door. There were children playing hopscotch beyond the wall, and he stopped and listened to them as his key turned in the lock; the taste of the Hoxton whisky was still in his mouth and he smiled and shook his head. The garage contained not a car, but a variety of interesting items among which Mr Rasmussen browsed seriously. There was an attaché case lying on the stone floor, and he picked it up, dusted it down and laid it open beside him. Next he went searching among a pile of timber and rubber tyres at the garage's other end. He emerged with a number of wedge-shaped pieces of wood, like the quarters of a cheese, and what looked like a single length of iron, five feet long but which, by manipulating the various sections of which it was constructed, he managed to reduce to a fifth of its original size.

Wood and iron now stowed in the attaché case, Mr Rasmussen paused and raised his head to see if he heard anything, but there was no sound except the muffled shouts of the children playing hopscotch thirty feet away. From a hiding place under a pile of newspapers he unearthed a couple of short, long-toothed saws. These, too, went into the attaché case, which was now so full that it required a considerable effort on Mr Rasmussen's part to induce the two edges to meet and close. In the end, though, the job was done, and Mr Rasmussen stood once more in the empty courtyard, the garage door locked behind him and the attaché case grasped firmly in his left hand. Having been so absorbed in his work, he was surprised to find that only forty minutes had passed since he had left Soho, but there it was. Somewhere to the north of him a roar of human voices—thousands of them, it seemed—was flung at him over the rooftops and he realized that he was in earshot of Highbury football ground, where the Arsenal game would be coming to an end. He took a bus back to the West End, sat amongst the football supporters with the attaché case balanced on his knees, and treated himself to fish and chips in a Lyons Corner House—it was the closest he would get to the salmon of the Solent—and then set off east along High Holborn, past Chancery Lane and Ludgate Circus, into the heart of the City.

12

SEIZING THE MOMENT

Sound Advice for the Salesman: VII. Strategy

Salesmen! Remember that the most successful operators are invariably those who study the sale from every angle. What does the customer want? Can you provide it? If not, is there something else you can offer which may be equally acceptable? Should the customer hesitate, what persuasion can you employ to clinch the deal? The strategy of the successful salesman may be compared to the strategy of the successful military campaign: forward planning; tactics; and ability to deal with the unexpected. Think of yourself as a Field Marshall whose moment of triumph is symbolized not by the blowing of trumpets but by the satisfied smile on the customer's face!

Abraxas Salesman's Handbook

If there was one thing the army had taught me, it was the value of preparation. Even that time when half a sack of mail went missing from the orderly room and I got hauled up in front of the Brigade Major, the corporal who put a word in for me said I had 'a very methodical approach to my work.' Fact is, I knew that if I was going anywhere near Newcome Grange, I'd need to make plans. It wasn't the kind of place you could just swan into as if it

157

was gala night at the Florida. Plus I'd be going there under false pretences, which made things even more difficult. For one thing, I'd need money. The train fare wouldn't pay for itself and then there'd be taxis and tips for servants. I knew all about country living, you see, even if it'd only been picked up in the kind of books where Gwendolyn's been invited down to Mallory Towers for the weekend by her young man—only the poor girl's got a spot on her nose. Anyway, all that week and the following one I slaved away on the door-to-door with the carpet lotion. Bayswater was pretty much played out by now—I'd been up and down the streets so often the housewives were sick of the sight of me—so after a day or two I tried a new beat in Golders Green, which wasn't so bad except for the tube fares and having to lug the kit up and down the underground steps. I'd got the patter off to a tee by now—I could eye up a customer, like a tailor measuring a bloke for a suit, and instantly decide what sort of line she'd fall for, and by the end of the first week I was averaging ten bob a day.

It was getting well on into September now and the pavements were wet underfoot. Up in Golders Green they were making bonfires out of the swept-up leaves and there were already kids on the street corners asking penny for the guy. Somehow, though, even with the Newcome Grange trip looming and the weekend with Susie gleaming in the distance beyond, I had this kind of sinking feeling dragging me down. Autumn always gives me the blues, you see. It's the time when all the pleasures you've chased in summer finally have to be paid for. Worse, it's the time when women take a good look at you and decide they might do better elsewhere. Netta'd given me the chuck in September. To add to this the financial crisis was getting worse, and you couldn't open a paper without seeing Montagu Norman marching into Number Ten or reading a piece by some chap worrying about the Gold Standard. Normally I don't take much interest in politics—I'd only voted once, in 1929, and went for the Communist because he looked such a sad little chap—but you could see that things were going badly wrong—there were even rumours about the Fleet being ready to mutiny—and that in the end we'd all have to pay for it.

So you can see I was in a cheery mood that fortnight, traipsing up and down the pavements of NW11 and making small-talk with the old women—they were mostly Jewish, and what they didn't know about haggling you could have written on the back of a pawn ticket. But there was four quid in the tobacco tin under the bed again, which meant I could think a bit about clothes. I had an old suit that I reckoned would just about do for the daytime, when I lolled around on Mrs Antrobus's sofas or took Susie for a stroll around the ha-ha, but I knew I'd never pass muster in the evening so I went to a shop I knew of in the Portobello Road and planked down thirty bob for the hire of a dinner jacket, some dress trousers—the kind that have a parallel groove running up the leg— and a wing collar. Then I spent the best part of an evening dabbing away at the remains of a pot of blacking I found in a cupboard, trying to make my shoes look respectable. When I'd finished I put the whole lot on, lit a fag and inspected myself in the mirror. Do you know, it wasn't half bad? Not

Ivor Novello going off to have dinner with Gertie Lawrence, maybe, but good enough for Newcome Grange.

Curiously enough, the easiest part of the business was squaring Mrs Fanshawe about her missing £3.15s. I'd been worrying about this for ages—there'd even been a couple of times when I'd pretended not to be in when she'd knocked at the door—and I reckoned that the best thing would be to make a clean breast of it. She wasn't such a bad sort, really: it's just that renting rooms to riff-raff makes you suspicious. Anyhow, I waited a while to pick my moment—her brother had taken to hanging round the place again and it couldn't be when he was there—and decided that I'd nip down to her sitting room one evening around seven. Sure enough, she was perched on the end of a cane chair listening to *Variety Bandbox* on the radio, with an aspidistra and a photo of a grim-looking bloke who I suspected was the late Mr Fanshawe for company, and seemed happy enough to see me.

'I wonder if I might have a word, Mrs Fanshawe?'

'Certainly, Mr Ross.'

Politeness always went a long way with Mrs F. A moment later I was comfortably installed in an armchair with a glass of sherry at my elbow—jolly good sherry it was—looking at a line of china racehorses that cantered across a pair of occasional tables and telling her about the little difficulty I was experiencing.

'As I'm sure you'll understand, Mrs Fanshawe,' I said, laying it on with a trowel, 'when one moves in certain circles one is always putting one's hand in one's pocket.'

'I do understand, Mr Ross.' Needless to say, the mention of country weekends had quite charmed the old girl. 'My husband used to say—it was when he was managing the RAC Club—that these days any kind of social position is simply an excuse for people to take advantage of you.'

'I'm sorry that I never had the opportunity of meeting your husband, Mrs Fanshawe. He sounds a very interesting man.'

'And of course nothing has ever been the same since the war.'

'I don't suppose it has.'

Mrs Fanshawe was on her second glass of sherry by now. I wondered what sort of a life she had here under the sickly aspidistra with Mr F staring at her out of his gunmetal frame.

'I think my husband would have liked you, Mr Ross. He was a great believer in courtesy, you see.'

'It costs nothing, Mrs Fanshawe.'

And so on for another twenty minutes, by which time I'd persuaded her to smoke a cigarette— she did this in a surprisingly expert manner—and agree an instalment plan for the £3.15s to run up to the week before Christmas, which was slightly longer than eternity in my book. I went back to my room thinking things were going as well as they could be. Outside there was fog creeping up over the hedge and the damp trees beyond and I wondered about heading into town for an evening at the Wheatsheaf. On the other hand, an evening at the Wheatsheaf would cost ten bob. Besides, there were other things I needed to do. A bit later I nipped out of the house—the sound of Henry Hall and his band was coming out from beneath Mrs Fanshawe's door by now—and made my way down to the phone box outside the pub then dialled the number Haversham had given me. I had this odd kind of feeling that Haversham might have forgotten about me, or not thought the game worth pursuing, but no, he knew who I was all right. Dead keen to see me, too, so we fixed to meet in a pub in Holborn the following night. I was late getting back from Golders Green, as it turned out, and by the time I'd stowed my kit at the office, accepted one of Hastings' cigarettes and told him what I thought of Mary Webb, it was so late I half-hoped he'd given it up as a bad job. But no, there he was, still in the same mackintosh, trilby hat tilted back on his forehead, perched on a stool by the bar with an inch of bitter in the pint glass by his elbow and cigarette smoke from the fag in his other hand crinkling up over his fingers.

'You're late,' he said, when he saw me.

There was an advert for Abdulla on the wall above his head, and I looked at the row of silly young faces while I answered him.

'Up in Golders Green,' I said. 'Couldn't get away.'

'Make anything much?'

'Ten bob.'

Oddly enough he seemed quite pleased to see me, despite being nearly stood up. The barman was standing by and he ordered another couple of pints, but as I made to take mine he slid his palm over the rim of the glass.

'This one's conditional,' he explained. 'What have you got?'

So I told him about the weekend at Newcome Grange, where I'd be sharing a house with Rasmussen and, as I relayed the facts of the case,

162

could really keep an eye on him. Naturally enough I didn't tell him about Susie. As I'd expected, he just lapped it up, together with the beer, at least two-thirds of which had disappeared by the time I'd finished telling him about the pilfered invite.

'That's a neat bit of work,' he said. 'Very neat. Sure you won't get found out?'

'She's never seen Jimmy before. If there's anyone there knows him, I'll just have to make some excuse. Say he told me to represent him, or something.'

'A neat bit of work,' Haversham said again. 'We could do with you on the force.' His eyes, once they'd stopped moving about, were quite dead, I noticed.

'Don't mind my asking,' I said, 'but what are you after him for?'

Haversham lowered his head and put his mouth to within a couple of inches of my ear. Close-up he smelled of smoke, beer and something else— mouthwash, perhaps, or peppermints. 'Jewel thief.'

'Go on!' For a moment I thought he was pulling my leg, but Haversham pulled the trilby off his head—it was the first time I'd ever seen him without it—clawed wildly at the sparse, pepper-and-salt hair beneath, jammed it back on again and made a shushing noise.

'Straight up. Furriers on Finsbury Pavement last month. Shop in the City just the other day.'

'He's not coming to Newcome Grange to lift Mrs Antrobus's diamonds, surely?'

'Who knows?'

'Why can't you arrest him now? Save all this trouble?'

Save all my trouble was what I meant.

'No evidence. Well, not much,' Haversham said. 'Shouldn't be telling you all this. More than my job's worth.' It struck me that I didn't actually know what his job was. 'But you just keep an eye on him, quiet like—what he says, who he talks to—and then you and me can say goodbye to each other and no questions asked.'

'Amen to that,' I said. We were getting on so well now that I squinted at the empty glasses and said: 'You want the other half of that?'

'Don't mind if I do.'

There was a little clip on his tie that I spotted for a Buffalo insignia. While I got the drinks he unrolled a copy of the *Star* and looked a bit mournfully at the front page, where the headline talked about the government sending out for a £250 million loan from New York.

'What d'you reckon about all this?' he asked, tapping the paper with the edge of his thumb.

'Don't know much about it.'

'All to do with the war if you ask me. Nothing gone right since then.'

Well, it was a point of view. 'Don't suppose it has,' I said.

He'd downed three pints by now. Unless, of course, the one he'd been finishing when I'd turned up had been his second, which meant four. At any rate it looked as if he and old Roper from the office could have given each other a run for their money. I stared a bit more at the Abdulla ad until the row of evening suits reminded me that was what was coming up at the weekend. Then Haversham fixed me with another look, rather as if in the intervening minute or two he'd forgotten who I was.

'I suppose you're too young to have fought in the

164

war?'

'Clerk in the postal service.' I explained about the hut on the Downs above Brighton with the kettle going in the background and Lance Corporal Hardcastle steaming open the mail.

'Oh well, them sort of things've got to be done,' Haversham said. 'You did your bit, I reckon.'

Something struck me and I said: 'You nick a chap called Callender recently?'

Haversham went all sphinx-like. 'Might have done. Why?'

'Used to work with him.'

'Bit of jiggery-pokery down Bognor way was what I heard,' Haversham said. 'Opened an electrical shop, stocked it up to the rafters, had a sale and then skedaddled on the proceeds with all the bills owing.'

'I just wondered.'

So old Callender had been on the long-firm game. It just went to show how you could never tell about people. Like Mrs Bence-Jones, who was a colonel's daughter, damn it, and had been to Cheltenham Ladies' College. Somehow all the stuff about Callender, and the sight of Haversham sinking his pint with those mad eyes of his staring out of his face, had sent my nerves jangling like piano wires. For two pins I'd have chucked the whole thing—even the chance of being with Susie— on the spot.

'What if I won't go?' I found myself asking.

Haversham gave a little nod over the rim of his beer glass, as if he'd half-expected this.

'Oh, you'll go all right.'

'Why's that then?'

'Otherwise a friend of mine at the tax office'll be

taking an interest in what you might or might not have been earning this past month or so. Get the picture?'

I got the picture. There was no way out of it, which was quite a compliment, when you thought about it, to my ingenuity in fixing it up. Anyway, I told Haversham I'd be in touch and he gave me a little salute, with two fingers flicked up to the brim of his hat. When I looked back he was perched on his stool by the bar again and ordering up another pint.

Next morning I totted up my resources and, would you believe it, I had nearly four quid. There wasn't much doing in Golders Green and the rain was coming down something fearful so I knocked off work early, found a phone box and rang the number on Jimmy's invitation card. A deferential male voice answered—the butler, I presumed—and, putting on the toniest accent I could muster, I announced that I was Mr James Carstairs and that I feared there might have been some mistake over my intentions with regard to Mrs Antrobus's house party and that I'd be delighted to come after all. The deferential male voice remarked that it would be pleased to convey this information to its mistress, and would I be coming from London, because if so the station to get off at was Haslemere. So that was that, and I walked out into the street thinking that this imposture business was a lot easier than people made out. In fact I was so bucked that I wondered about going into one of those little print shops in Holborn and having some cards made up with Jimmy's name on them, but something told me that this was probably illegal whereas ringing somebody up and pretending to be somebody else might just get filed under the heading of practical joke.

All that happened on the Wednesday, and Mrs Antrobus's guests were bidden to assemble any time after Friday luncheon. For a bit I wondered about hanging around in Old Street to see if I could catch Susie when she came out of work, but something told me to keep my powder dry until the weekend. Instead I went to a florist's in Hampstead and had a dozen roses sent along with a note saying: *Greatly looking forward to seeing you, James.* You can't go wrong with flowers. Even Netta used to melt at the sight of a bunch of carnations.

And then, late on that Wednesday afternoon, something deuced odd happened. I was in Hastings' office reminding him that I wouldn't be about on the Friday and touching him for a couple of Gold Flake when he said: 'Come and have a drink.'

'It's only half-four. They're not open.'

'Not in a pub. Little place I know.'

'Where's that then?'

'You'll see.'

That was all he'd let on, and so we strolled out of the office—there were a couple of brown envelopes with red stamps on them marked URGENT lying face-up on the carpet under the letter-box—in silence, dodged under the dripping trees (it had been raining again) and fetched up at the bus stop in High Holborn. 'Couple of tuppennies,' Hastings said to the conductor, when the bus pulled in, giving me a wink as he did so, and I realized I'd seen that kind of look before. It's that 'life in the old dog yet' look that middle-aged men give you when you catch them coming out of one of the rubber shops in Soho with a copy of *High Jinks in a Parisian Convent* by Sadie Blackeyes. Anyway, Hastings still wouldn't say anything, so I sat quiet beside him staring out at the wet streets and the crowds of people going by, picking out faces: a tall bloke with a sandwich board saying the end of the world had come; a mousy girl in a beret with a Pekingese under her arm; a chap in a morning coat with a buttonhole, who'd clearly mislaid his chauffeur somewhere. They don't look happy, those London crowds, but do they have any reason to be? We were about a quarter mile down Oxford Street, just in sight of Bourne & Hollingsworth, where the Old Lady used to buy her bedspreads, when Hastings danced up from his seat and said: 'This here's our stop.' Anyhow, I followed him off the bus, took a left into Poland Street and a couple of rights through an alleyway— Hastings seemed mightily familiar with the route, I noticed—and came out in a kind of dingy courtyard with a door set back in the wall and a sign saying: PEGASUS CLUB: *Members Only*.

'Chap I know told me about this,' Hastings said. 'Nice little place.'

Well, I've been in those Soho clip-joints before, and I reckoned we'd be lucky if we found a couple of card tables and a waitress selling bottles of dandelion and burdock. But no, whoever ran the Pegasus Club evidently knew what he was about. There was a nigger on the door got up in an evening suit and a dicky bow, who waved us up the staircase as if we were visiting royalty, two or three girls who looked as if they'd stepped out of the adverts in *Country Life* rather than being dragged off the pavement in Meard Street half-an-hour before, and the whisky was only eighteen pence a go. Why on earth Hastings wanted to come here I couldn't for the life of me fathom, but I could think of worse ways of spending my time.

'Here's how,' Hastings said, clinking his whisky glass against mine.

'Here's how.' It was real whisky, too, not like you get in some of the Soho places.

'It's nearly five o'clock,' I said, by way of conversation. 'Don't you have to go back and shut up the office?'

'B——y office can look after itself,' Hastings said. 'Caretaker locks up.'

I looked round the room we were sitting in, the walls of which were covered in what looked like surrealist paintings (I'd read an article about this in the *New Statesman* and knew some of the jargon), but there was no one much about. A couple of likely lads in mauve suits were jamming pennies into a fruit machine, one of the girls was perched on a stool by the bar trying to mend a ladder in her stocking, and a chap in plus fours with an Old Bill moustache was sitting on his own in the corner reading a book called *With Rod and Line through Argyllshire*. Just an ordinary afternoon in Soho, in fact.

'Interesting people you meet round here,' Hastings said. 'Not just the girls, I mean.'

'How's Mrs Hastings?' I asked.

'Actually,' Hastings said, 'we've got my mother-inlaw staying with us at the moment, if you take my meaning.'

'That's bad.'

'B——y bad, I'd call it.'

All this time I'd been staring at the girl perched on the bar stool who was trying to mend the ladder in her stocking, while I thought about

169

Susie and the weekend and what sort of story I could manufacture for Haversham, but just at that moment, as Hastings was telling me some more about his mother-in-law and how she plundered the sherry when she thought no one was looking, I got one hell of a shock. You see, the girl was Marjorie. I hadn't seen her for a couple of years, but there was no mistaking that droopy under-lip and the way she had of blinking her eyes a dozen times a minute—she was very short-sighted—whenever she looked up. What was Marjorie doing in a place like the Pegasus? The last time I'd seen her she'd been working as lady-companion to an old girl in Belgrave Square who was trying to start a donkey sanctuary in Andalucia. Anyway, while I was thinking all this, Hastings, who was well on to his second whisky, said:

'Of course, I daresay you think it's a bit of a comedown, chap like me doing a job like this.'

'We all have to earn a living.'

'You won't credit it, perhaps, but there was a time when I almost went into the Church.'

'What was it that stopped you?'

'You'd be surprised,' Hastings said. 'It wasn't just ordinary doubts or anything.'

'James,' Marjorie said suddenly. She'd finished mending the ladder in her stockings and was blinking wildly across the room. 'I thought it was you.'

'How are you Marjorie?' I said. For a moment I couldn't remember how we'd left each other two years before, but I knew it was nothing like the business with Netta. Nothing in the history of my dealings with women had been as bad as that. Anyhow, she didn't seem to harbour a grudge

170

because she breezed on:

'Fancy seeing you in a place like this.'

'What happened to Lady Kenmare?'

'Oh, she died. And then her nephew said that he didn't care if the donkeys were turned into cat food, so I came here . . . Aren't you going to introduce me to your friend?'

'This is Mr Hastings.'

'Claude,' Hastings said. It was the first time I'd heard his Christian name. 'Do I take it that you and this young lady are acquainted?'

'Mr Hastings nearly became a clergyman,' I said.

'I like spiritual men,' Marjorie said. I couldn't tell if she was guying him or not.

Pretty soon Hastings—he was on to his third whisky by now—was telling us exactly why he hadn't become a clergyman. It was something to do with what an archdeacon he knew had said to the rural dean, but I couldn't make it out: I was too busy thinking about Susie and whether the money I'd got saved would be enough. Marjorie must have twigged that my heart wasn't in it any more, because she tweaked the arm of my jacket and said:

'Quiet as the grave you are, James. Aren't you pleased to see me?'

'Not feeling too good,' I explained.

'And this was a man,' Hastings said—he was really animated now—'who thought it was tickety-boo to wear a Gothic cope with a modern Italian-lace alb.'

'Do you want me to get one of the girls to make you some scrambled eggs?'

'It's all right, thanks.'

It was nearly six o'clock. The Wheatsheaf would be open by now. It was only half a mile away, but I

171

knew I ought to get back to Mrs Fanshawe's.

'You must come and see us again,' Marjorie said as I got up to go. 'Wednesdays, Saturdays and Sundays is when I'm here. Other times I'm mostly at the Blue Lantern in Ham Yard.'

'I'll try and remember,' I said. Hastings was sitting tilted backwards in his chair with his mouth half-open, staring at one of the surrealist paintings. He didn't respond when I nodded at him.

In ordinary circumstances I suppose I'd have been interested in coming across Marjorie again, and finding out more about what had stopped Hastings from becoming a clergyman, but funnily enough none of it seemed to mean anything. Come the Thursday I didn't work much beyond lunchtime. After that I went and sat in the Wheatsheaf and wondered just exactly what I was getting myself into. All the sparkle had gone out of it somehow. What would Susie say when she saw me? And what was I supposed to say to Mrs Antrobus? And how did you greet a suspected jewel thief you were supposed to be shadowing? It was a measure of how low I'd got that I ended up in a coffee shop in Wardour Street with old Parkinson, listening to him tell me about his mother and how she'd been one of the Plymouth Brethren and made him go to sleep in a kind of chastity belt in case he galloped the antelope during the night.

Next morning there was rain falling in torrents over the Paddington squares and the trees were full of bedraggled pigeons huddling up for shelter. Funnily enough I felt a whole lot better. The wireless news, which I listened to while I was shaving, said the Cabinet was meeting to discuss spending cuts, but I didn't let it spoil the kick I was feeling at the prospect of the day ahead. By nine o'clock I had my clothes laid out in the suitcase I'd borrowed from Mrs Fanshawe and the poem I'd written for Susie—I'd finished this a couple of nights ago—in the inside pocket of my coat and was ticking off expenses in my head. Train ticket thirteen-and-six (I'd bought this in advance at Waterloo the day before). Taxis say six bob both ways—I had an idea Newcome Grange was about three miles from Haslemere, but you never knew. Tips for the servants—I'd play that by ear, but it might be as much as ten bob all round and another ten bob for the butler. When I'd done this two or three times it was still only half-past nine, but I knew that if I didn't set out now I'd only loaf about the place kicking my heels in misery, so I picked up Mrs Fanshawe's case—a superior item it was, too, in brown imitation leather—shut the door behind me and strode off down the staircase. Looking back over the past few months—meeting Susie, working on the door-to-door, spending the night in the waiting room at King's Cross—I had the odd feeling that everything had been leading up to this point. I couldn't quite work out why, but there was no denying the chain of consequences: I'd got caught up in something I couldn't get out of and now here I was off to Waterloo under false pretences with three quid in my pocket and nothing much across the horizon except debt and bottles of carpet lotion. Apart from Susie, that was. I'd been keeping that letter she'd sent me in my jacket pocket, and now I pulled it out again. *Hoping we can be together very soon.* A girl wouldn't write that unless she was really gone on you, would she? Outside in the street the rain had stopped, the sun had come out and the pavements were sparkling beneath odd flashes of light. I could see the clouds marching off towards the west. Well, that was all right. It was a bit like this whole business of the Gold Standard, really. Just for once, somebody else was in for a packet.

13

NIGHT AND THE CITY

The 'Corinthian' safe designed by Messrs Milner at the express solicitation of the firm of Singleton & Keating jewellers, of Lower Cornhill may be warmly recommended. Of solid steel plate to a depth of two inches, the lock—constructed by Messrs Chubb—consisting of a brass front with reinforced steel spiders, its manufacturers are confident that no more secure repository has yet been placed before the public.

Locksmith's Gazette, *September 1931*

Davenport and Hines, waiting on the corner of Finsbury Square in the early twilight, did not see him until he appeared under their noses. But there he was suddenly among them, the attaché case swinging in his gloved hand. 'Startled us, mooching up like that,' Davenport protested. Hines was more matter-of-fact about these things. They set off across the square in single file, the spaces between them so emphatic that anyone observing their progress might have doubted that they had any connection with each other. The carpet-bag that

174

Hines carried was clearly a trouble to him, for he stopped every so often and transferred it from one arm to the other and swore sharply when the handle chafed his wrist. The march continued for some moments, along Lothbury to Threadneedle Street, westward into Cornhill. Here Mr Rasmussen said something to his companions that caused them to draw back and take an interest in the front window of a flower shop. Looking first to his left and then to his right, and finding no one in sight, Mr Rasmussen walked casually along Cornhill until he came to the street door of the laundry.

As he had anticipated, it was locked. Producing the thin metal cylinder he had used on his previous visit, he inserted this into the lock, gave a neat little twist with his fingers and passed through rapidly into the entry hall beyond. Before him, dimly visible in the shadow, the staircase ran up into darkness. If Mr Rasmussen's features had betrayed any anxiety during this manoeuvre, they now relaxed. Making sure that the door was pushed almost to behind him, he took a torch out of his pocket and shone its beam of light up the stairs. They were coated with dust: clearly no one had been there since he had last walked up them himself. There was a noise of movement behind him—footsteps, hands scrabbling at the door—and Davenport and Hines joined him breathlessly in the hallway. Mr Rasmussen pushed the door shut, picked up a boot-scraper that lay by the inner door of the laundry and jammed it up against the wood. 'There,' he said. 'No one can disturb us.' They moved on up the staircase, their boots resounding on the steps.

'You see,' Mr Rasmussen said, as if he were explaining some elementary point of mathematics, 'it is really very simple.' The door of the defunct tea-brokers was exactly as he had left it, except that the TO LET sign had become even more dirt-strewn. Mr Rasmussen worked on the lock for a moment, listened to the little crack that it made as it came apart and pushed it open: the mice went skittering away across the floor. In contrast to his previous visit, Mr Rasmussen did not linger in the vestibule or shine his torch—the beam kept low and allowed to rise no more than a few inches from the floor—into the first set of offices. He made straight for the room where he had examined the set of wicker baskets and smelled the jasmine. Here there was only a single window, hidden under blinds, and he let the torch-beam play over the interior.

Davenport and Hines watched him as he worked, keen to place their expertise at his disposal. 'So this here's the gaff?' Hines asked, throwing down the carpet-bag with a thump that suggested whatever lay inside it was very heavy indeed.

'Shush,' Mr Rasmussen said. 'We'll be making enough noise later, I daresay. This is the gaff. Directly above the strongroom.'

'So do we go down here?' Davenport enquired.

In answer, Mr Rasmussen lifted up a corner of the carpet and, just as he had done on that previous visit, stamped his foot hard on the boards. This time there was a dull ringing sound. 'Metal plate,' Mr Rasmussen observed. 'They've reinforced the ceiling. No, we'll go next door and come through the tobacconist's beyond. There are two rooms, front and back. The shop itself and a storeroom. If we pick our spot, we can come down through the storeroom.'

It was beautiful to watch Mr Rasmussen at work.

Arriving in the furthermost room—windowless, and allowing the torch-beam to be played to its fullest extent—he took off his jacket and hung it over the photograph of Queen Mary in her coronation robes, almost as if he did not wish that lady to see what he was doing. Then, instructing Hines to remove the carpet, he opened the attaché case, took out a piece of chalk from a canvas bag that lay there and drew four straight lines on the wood, forming a square the sides of which might have been eighteen inches long. All this Davenport watched with interest. One of the heavy objects that the carpet-bag contained turned out to be a short hatchet, and with this he aimed a single blow at a corner of the square that Mr Rasmussen indicated with his hand. There was a rending sound, but muffled, the point of the hatchet passing quickly through the wood and burying itself in the plaster beneath.

'Hines,' Mr Rasmussen said, almost conversationally, 'just go back to the main staircase, would you, and see that the coast is clear?' They listened to his footfalls disappearing along the corridor, and then resumed their work. Taking one of the saws, Mr Rasmussen inserted it into the crevice made by the hatchet and began, methodically, to cut his way around the perimeter of the square. As he did this, Davenport followed him with a crow bar, also produced from the carpet-bag, with which he tore up the boards, exposing the plaster beneath to view.

Perhaps half an hour went by in this way, Mr Rasmussen alternately sawing and rubbing his sawing hand with his fingers, Davenport prising the pieces of wood out of the hole and conveying them to the corner of the room. Hines padded back along the corridor, the doors banging softly in his wake, and watched them, hunkering down on his heels. 'Di tell you,' Davenport asked, heaping up another pile of fragments in his arms, 'bout that job me and Silvester done in Camden?'

'No,' Mr Rasmussen replied, politely, but giving the faint impression that Davenport was sometimes a trial to him, 'you did not tell me. What happened?' Nearly all the wood was gone now, and the plaster gleamed dully from the hole.

'I'd got out into the street,' Davenport said. 'But Silvester's still in the 'all when the Jimmy who owns the gaff come back. Jimmy says: "What's all this then?" And Silvester says: "Is this the post office?" What a mulligatawny, eh?'

'Careful with that,' Mr Rasmussen admonished. 'We don't want the ceiling coming down.' He took a hammer from the carpet-bag and tapped briskly at the plaster. They heard the faint thuds as the flakes fell into the room below. 'What time is it?' Mr Rasmussen demanded. It was about half-past eight. Already they seemed to have been hours in the room. 'Well, we are in no hurry,' Mr Rasmussen assured them. 'We can stay all night if we have to.'

'F—— that,' Hines said. 'Booked for Sunday.'

'What you doing?' Davenport asked.

'F——g church parade with the boy scouts isn't it?' Hines told him.

The square of the floor from which the boards and the plaster had been torn out was gaping and empty. Mr Rasmussen shone his torch into the hole. 'Storeroom,' he said. 'A nine-foot drop, perhaps.'

There was a rusting metal cabinet, mounted on

castors, in one of the rooms, and they wheeled it up next to the hole and secured the coil of rope that Hines produced from the carpet-bag to one of its stanchions. Davenport took the other end of the rope, flung it through the hole and lowered himself gently through. A moment later the three of them were standing in the tobacconist's storeroom, brushing the fragments of plaster from their clothes and shining Mr Rasmussen's torch over the shelves of tobacco jars and chocolate. 'Ja see that?' Davenport said. 'Two hundred packets of Gold Flake if there's one. See if I don't catch some of that before we go.'

'Gold Flake,' Hines said. 'What you want Gold Flake for when you can have f——g cigars?'

Mr Rasmussen, meanwhile, had dropped to his knees and was examining the near-hand wall of the room, administering sundry little taps with the knuckles of his right fist and inclining an ear to register the impression they produced. Somewhere above his head there was a rasp, an inhalation of breath and a rich smell of tobacco smoke. 'For God's sake,' said Mr Rasmussen, a shade less amiably than before, 'put that out will you? Do you know how far it carries?'

Davenport extinguished his cigar on his boot sole, grinning broadly. 'We going in there?' he asked, tapping the wall.

'Seems to me that there's another plate,' Mr Rasmussen said. 'But no harm checking. Give me that, will you?' With the help of the light hammer Hines had given him, he twisted a nail out of an exposed beam that ran lengthways across the far wall. Placing the nail in his left hand—it was perhaps six inches long—he drove it smartly into the plaster of the nearside wall, withdrew the blunted end and displayed it under the light of the torch.

As he did this, he was calculating. It seemed to him likely that the tobacconist's premises would possess a cellar, and quite as likely that it would adjoin the cellar that he believed to exist beneath the floor of the jeweller's strongroom. The question was: how far beneath ground level did the jeweller's reinforcements extend? By shining the beam of his torch towards the back of the room and putting his shoulder to a couple of packing cases, Mr Rasmussen discovered a trapdoor. This revealed a second room, smaller than the storeroom in which they stood, with a rough, concrete floor, empty except for a few rolls of sacking. There was no need for secrecy here, Mr Rasmussen thought. He took the torch and placed it in a cranny in the wall. Silently he inspected the cellar. As he had suspected, the nearside wall was of red brick. Tapping it with the light hammer, he decided that it was not thick—perhaps two or three bricks in diameter. Also, he fancied that much of the brickwork was in poor repair: there were great stretches where it had hollowed out to a depth of two or three inches, and the floor was thick with brick dust.

It then occurred to him that his security, and to a lesser extent that of his colleagues, was paramount during this operation. Accordingly, he instructed Davenport to make his way into the front of the tobacconist's shop and ensure that nothing untoward was going on in the street, and sent Hines back to the upper room from which they had made their original descent to collect the carpet-bag. While they did this, Mr Rasmussen once again inspected the brickwork, nudged at it with his hammer and once or twice picked at the mortar with his forefinger. It certainly was very uneven. He looked at his watch and found that it was about half-past nine. He could not account for how the time had passed. It was a mystery to him where it had gone. Presently Davenport came back from the shop and reported that, concealed behind the till, he had watched a policeman pass the door, shine his torch in at the window and then move on. A moment or so later Hines joined them with the carpet-bag slung over his shoulder. Mr Rasmussen thought very hard about the task that lay before him. The passing hours did not concern him. He knew that he had until dawn on Monday morning, if he needed the time. What did concern him, even here, twelve feet underground and another twenty feet from the pavement, was the possibility of his being overheard.

But Mr Rasmussen had an idea—having taken a lively interest in the methods of the City police—that the officer who had shone his torch in at the window of the tobacconist's shop had a beat that took him as far as London Wall and, therefore, had a good many other torch-shinings and door-tuggings to accomplish; he could not be expected to return for another hour. 'We had better do this as quickly as we can,' he announced, picking up the carpet-bag and reaching into it. The reason for Hines's difficulty in carrying it now became apparent, for the bag contained a pair of 20lb hammers, as well as a number of iron spikes eight or nine inches in length. One of them Mr Rasmussen now set into a gap in the brick and, seizing one of the hammers, drove it in as far as he could. This manoeuvre, repeated two or three times, produced a loosening of the surrounding stone, which Davenport, attacking it with the other hammer, was able to enlarge to a depth of three or four inches.

Looking at the hole, Mr Rasmussen was satisfied with what he saw. But the noise of the hammers seemed to him extraordinarily loud. Never mind. He calculated that they had fifty minutes until the policeman, now far away at the end of Cornhill, passed the shop doorway again. Still, he could not rid himself of the thought of the torch shining at the door of the tobacconist's shop. Leaving Davenport and Hines to continue belabouring the bricks, he made his way back to the storeroom and through a connecting door to the shop, crouching down so that, even if anyone should be passing the window, he could not be seen. Rising to his feet again and remaining there, motionless, like a waxwork in the gloaming, he peered out into Cornhill, but there was no one there, just an occasional vehicle passing in the middle of the road, forty feet away. He realized that he was acutely conscious of the noise of the hammers, and yet he imagined that the disturbance would not perhaps be audible from the street, and that even if it was audible, there would be nothing to connect it with the premises in which they stood. Cheered by this, he went back to the cellar, where Davenport and Hines, very red-faced and covered in brick dust, were smoking cigarettes and contemplating a small hole that had now appeared in the brick, and through which cold air—colder than the air of the room in which they stood—was now seeping. 'That's the mulligatawny,'

Davenport said.

Mr Rasmussen inspected the hole, put his torch into it, played the torch-beam through it and assured himself that his calculation about the adjoining cellars had been correct. While Davenport and Hines smoked their cigarettes, he made various efforts to enlarge the hole, tugging out pieces of brickwork and shards of mortar. 'Dear me,' he said mildly. 'We shall have the whole wall down on us if we don't take care.'

'Stick of dynamite,' Hines suggested. 'That'd settle it.'

'And us too,' said Mr Rasmussen, who did not quite trust Davenport and Hines and was thinking that at the close of this particular excursion he might very well forget the way to the Pegasus Club. It was by now about eleven o'clock, and another half-hour's work would enlarge the hole to the point where the three of them, together with the carpet-bag and the attaché case, could make their way through into the adjoining room.

Here there were fewer obstacles to their progress. A flight of wooden steps led up to a door (unlocked) that admitted them to a passageway at the back of the jeweller's premises. The faint glow of a street-lamp indicated the position of the showroom, but to the left, a few feet along the corridor, was a large, reinforced door with an iron surround. This Mr Rasmussen knew to be the strongroom. Bending down, with the light of the torch half concealed in the palm of his hand, he inspected the lock, ran his hand up and down the door frame above and beneath it and rapped here and there with his fist.

'Hammers?' Davenport suggested, his face

183

looming up through the dark.

'And wake every caretaker between here and Liverpool Street?' Mr Rasmussen lectured him. 'Certainly not.'

Picking up the attaché case, he selected a thin piece of metal, not unlike a button-hook in design, and inserted it into the lock, listening all the while to the sound of its effect on the interior mechanism. He repeated this procedure three or four times, finally requesting Hines, braced in the passage behind him, to kick the door frame as hard as he could. The lock broke and they fell into the strongroom.

There was an electric light switch on the wall by his shoulder, and Mr Rasmussen, having shut the door carefully behind him, depressed it, flooding the room with bright, artificial light. The safe lay on a metal plate in the corner—apart from a row of cabinets on the opposite wall, it was the only object in there—but Mr Rasmussen hesitated to approach. He stood for a moment getting his bearings. The absence of any noise whatever, aside from their breathing and the squeal of their boots on the iron floor suggested that the plate-metal walls offered the incidental benefit of soundproofing. Still, though, he was not satisfied. Turning off the light and opening the door half a foot or so, he sent Hines out into the showroom to inspect the street beyond. There was no one there, Hines reported, jaunty now that they had reached the object of their mission. Mr Rasmussen said that he was glad to hear it. Inspecting the safe—it had a blue-grey metal surface and was about four feet by three—he saw, as he had anticipated, that it had been made by Messrs Milner and displayed a lock patented by Messrs Chubb.

Mr Rasmussen frowned. He knew he would get nowhere with that lock, and that a manoeuvre that might in ordinary circumstances have taken a few minutes and been accomplished by guile would now take several hours and require brute force. Still, he produced his button-hook and gave a twist or two, in case by some miracle the lock might be faulty. It was not.

Davenport and Hines, he saw, were regarding him sardonically. All the previous expertise he had shown, he realized, was nothing to them. He gave the safe a last little tap with the finger of his glove.

'You need a bly,' Hines suggested.

'And three days' leisure, perhaps,' Mr Rasmussen said, rather tartly, 'if you want to burn through two inches of steel.'

He took the attaché case, laid it open on the floor before him, and took out a tiny wedge of iron, no more than three inches long and tapering to a sharp point, held it to the point where the door met the wall of the safe, perhaps a foot above the lock, and gave half-a-dozen taps with the light hammer. Inspecting the result, he found the wedge had created a gap between door and wall of perhaps an eighth of an inch. For nearly half an hour Mr Rasmussen laboured in this way, taking thin strips of metal out of the case and driving them into the safe with his hammer. When he had finished he played the torch-beam on the door and assured himself that the gap six or eight inches above the lock had widened to a depth of perhaps a quarter of an inch.

Into this aperture he was able to fit the end of one of the wooden wedges. To succeed in widening the gap any further would, he knew, require a full-scale assault on the safe, and the disturbance that this would create alarmed him. Accordingly, he sent Hines back into the showroom with instructions to return if the slightest movement should be glimpsed beyond the window. This done, and sweating profusely from the exertions of the previous half-hour, he indicated to Davenport that he should set about the wedge with one of the 20lb hammers. Davenport struck a couple of blows, whereupon Mr Rasmussen stopped him, examined the position of the wedge, ran his eye along the door and then told him to recommence. Gradually, this had the makings of a routine: Davenport driving the wedge home; Mr Rasmussen making minor interventions and adjustments, and then urging him to proceed.

All this went on for nearly an hour. Above their heads they could hear a clock sounding midnight. Mr Rasmussen called a halt and inspected the damage done. It was considerable. A fissure had opened in the top of the safe that was perhaps an inch and a half wide, but he knew that there was as yet no prospect of the lock breaking. Hines came back from the showroom and was informed by Davenport that there was no chance of his going to his f——g church parade. Mr Rasmussen smiled, with an amiability he did not quite feel, took another wooden wedge from the carpet-bag, fitted it into the fissure and nodded to Davenport to strike at it. 'Be here all f——g night,' Hines complained.

Mr Rasmussen thought of the iron bar in his attaché case, but knew that its use would be premature, that the hole in the safe was not sufficiently wide for it to be inserted. And so they went on for another half-hour: a blow or two from Davenport, an adjustment from Mr Rasmussen, another blow, another adjustment. Calling a further halt, Mr Rasmussen found that the gap between the wall and the upper part of the door of the safe had now widened to a depth of two inches, so that he could see the edge of one of the metal trays within. 'What's in there, anyhow?' Davenport asked, resting the hammer on the toe of his boot. 'Perishing crown jewels?'

'I think you'll find what's in there will repay our labour,' Mr Rasmussen told him, thinking of the conversation in Mrs Antrobus's drawing room.

'What's that?' Hines demanded suddenly, cocking his head. Instantly they fell silent. Mr Rasmussen thought that he could hear nothing, that he had never known a silence like it, down here in the depths of Cornhill, but he was aware that his senses had been dulled by the clamour of the past hour and a half. Switching off the electric light and plunging the strongroom into darkness, he sent Hines on all fours along the passage to see if there was any disturbance at the front of the shop. Hines, padding back on all fours, reported that there was a policeman shining his torch into the showroom window. Mr Rasmussen found himself calculating furiously. He believed that the chance of anyone having heard any noise from the strongroom was minimal. However, he also knew that he could not continue in such circumstances, nor for some while beyond. Whispering to Davenport and Hines to keep silent, he crept out into the passage. There was moonlight shining on to the plaster, and a series of rattlings—faint but insistent—emanating

187

from the front of the shop. Mr Rasmussen understood this to mean that the policeman was trying the door-knob.

Still, he thought, this did not mean very much. The policeman, surely, would complete his investigations, assure himself that nothing was amiss and then depart, leaving Mr Rasmussen with the leisure to insert the iron bar into the fissure between the door and the wall of the safe. Not wanting to return to the strongroom just yet, for fear that his movements might attract attention, he crouched in the shadow of the wall. As he did this, though, he was aware that he was already calculating the ease, or otherwise, of their escape route: through the smashed wall of the jeweller's cellar and into the tobacconist's basement, on through the hole in the roof, back into the tea-broker's. But what if the police were watching the outer door of the laundry? Just as Mr Rasmussen was considering this possibility, there was a terrific bang away to his right. Not caring if he were heard, for he knew that the noise of the bang would have been audible from the street, Mr Rasmussen scuttled back into the strongroom. The light had been switched on and Davenport and Hines stood nervously contemplating a display case that had fallen from the shelves behind the safe. 'How on earth did this happen?' he demanded.

'Is full of watches isn't it?' Hines retorted, with a gesture at his accomplice. 'F——r was filling his pockets.'

Mr Rasmussen shot a glance at the case, the surface of which had been shattered with a hammer blow, its force clearly causing it to fall to the floor. Immediately he bent down, scooped up a handful of the watches and stuffed them into his attaché case. 'We must get out of here,' he instructed. 'Every policeman in the City will be here in a moment or two.'

It was all done in a second. The hammers went into the carpet-bag, and the metal bar—at which Davenport cast a regretful glance—followed. Hines dropped a watch under his feet, crushed it accidentally with his boot and swore. As they sped along the passage to the cellar steps, they heard a redoubled rattling and the sound of whistles blowing in the distance. The tobacconist's cellar was gathered up in shadow: above their heads the hole in the ceiling gaped, the darkness above it blacker still. 'Let's hope that f——g rope holds,' muttered Hines. Mr Rasmussen, listening all the while for sounds of pursuit, said he hoped so, too. Reaching the upper floor he sat back on his heels and trained the torch-beam back on his companions as they made their ascent. Of the two, Hines was the least adept. There was a moment when he hung dangling in mid-air as Mr Rasmussen and Davenport tugged manfully on the rope and a little shower of plaster fragments descended on his head. Then they were running through the tea-broker's corridor with the mice scampering to safety at their heels.

Reaching the far door, Mr Rasmussen motioned to them to be silent. 'If we go out through the street door, we shall be seen,' he explained. They broke silently through the inner door of the laundry, found the window that Mr Rasmussen had explored on his previous visit and lowered themselves into the alleyway beyond.

'Couple of dozen watches in there,' Davenport said, tapping his pocket. 'Not so bad.'

189

Mr Rasmussen thought of the contents of the safe, inwardly cursed his luck and politely agreed. A gust of raw air came springing up around the corner of the alleyway, a shaft of bitter light from a street-lamp fell over their heads and somewhere in the middle distance a clock struck one.

14

COUNTRY LIFE

Sound Advice for the Salesman: VIII. Triumph

Every so often there will dawn one of those bright, unheralded mornings in which all the hard work of the previous days and months will bear fruit. Did not our immortal bard observe that 'there is a tide in the affairs of men, which, taken at the flood, leads on to fortune'? He never spoke a truer word. Salesmen! If your sights are firmly set on the victory target then, when this moment comes, you cannot fail!

Abraxas Salesman's Handbook

Fact is, everything worked out according to plan. By half-past eleven I'd got down to Waterloo, bought a ticket (thirteen-and-six return) picked up twenty Sahib Virginia Straight Cut to see me through the weekend and a *Mirror* to read on the train—the headline said GOLD STANDARD: BANK TO ACT—and was bowling away on the 10.59 to Haslemere (change at Crystal Palace for intermediate stations to Dorking, and Guildford for the coastal service). Actually, I never looked at the paper. I was too busy staring out of the window at the Surrey countryside, which for some reason reminded me of Netta, and worrying how I'd get on. As I saw it the trick was not to get ruffled by anything, and if anyone turned nasty there was always the front door to scoot out of or even the drain-pipe to shin down.

As it turned out, I needn't have worried. The train sailed into Haslemere at 11.48 a.m. on the dot. It seemed a sleepy sort of place, just the kind of spot I could take Susie for our weekend, and I made a mental note to look for a pub that did rooms on the way back. All the taxis had gone from the station forecourt, but in the end I found a bloke in a pre-war Ford who offered to take me there for five bob. He was a cheery old soul and clearly a great one for the beer, and in normal circumstances I daresay we'd have got on like a house on fire, but somehow I didn't feel like talking much. Anyway, he prosed on about Mrs Antrobus—he knew all about her—and Newcome Grange, which, to great local displeasure, she'd redesigned after buying the old estate. The cow parsley rose up in the back lanes and the rain fell in sheets and I went over for the umpteenth time in my mind what I was going to say to people I was introduced to.

'What d'you make of this financial crisis?' the bloke asked at one point.

'Don't really know much about it,' I told him.

'Fifteen million quid the frogs are supposed to be ready to lend us.'

'That's a lot of money.'

'If it were me, I'd take it from the Germans. I

191

mean, who else's fault is it?'

'It's a point of view.'

Soon after this we turned off the road and went chugging through a kind of park, with deer huddled up under the trees, and the old bloke looked up from the wheel on which his head was practically resting and said, 'That's Newcome Grange, that is', and all the reassurances I'd been feeding myself up with, instead of breakfast, flew out of the window, for it was the swankiest place you ever saw, like something out of a film set, with wings stretching away on either side and a great gravel drive with a fountain in the middle. Five minutes later I was standing with my case on the steps, with the Ford swaying off into the distance—if you ask me the old chap was aiming to take my five bob straight off to the nearest pub—and the butler asking me: 'What name, sir?' and I was so light-headed that I damn near said 'James Ross' and only got the Carstairs out with a kind of last-second yelp while my real name was floating on the edge of my tongue.

Anyhow, the butler said that they were putting me in the west wing, that luncheon was at one and that I might find the other guests in the drawing room or possibly in the grounds, and it was so like a P.G. Wodehouse novel that I nearly asked if Lord Emsworth was round the back with one of his pigs. Instead I nodded gravely, said that was fine by me, oversaw the removal of my case (which didn't look at all bad in the footman's grasp), tipped that domestic a bob, bringing the morning's expenditure to a guinea, looked in a mirror to make sure that shirt, collar and tie were OK and that I'd shaved properly, and walked down to the drawing room. Here I had two worries. One was that there'd be someone there who knew Jimmy and would spot me for a fraud. The second was that there'd be someone with a working knowledge of the *Blue Bugloss*. I had a feeling, though, that culture of the kind represented by the *Blue Bugloss* wouldn't cut much ice in Mrs Antrobus's drawing room, and so it proved. In fact, from the looks on the faces of the people I went round shaking hands with, it could have been *Cage Birds* for all they cared. Then, just as I thought I could relax a bit, up pops a rickety-looking, pale-faced clergyman who said:

'Delighted to meet you, Mr Carstairs. I am one of your subscribers.'

I said I was delighted, too, and what part of the paper did he particularly like, and he said he especially admired F.S. Littlejohn's poems, so I racked my brains to remember what F.S. Littlejohn's poems were like—ghastly RC nature poetry, I seemed to recall—and said that no doubt we'd be putting some more of them in soon. I've watched editors at parties, you see, and this is how they talk.

All the time, though, I was casting anxious glances around the room in search of Susie. My real worry was that she and Rasmussen'd come in together, in which case I'd have a difficult job, but thankfully there was no sign of them. The clock was moving on towards one now, and one of the maids was banging a gong in the hall, and though I was half-starved I reckoned that it might not be a bad idea to skip lunch and lie low for a while. Then, by the grace of God, just as I was skulking off towards the main staircase I practically ran into her coming across the hall. She was wearing a blue two-piece and didn't look at all like somebody's secretary:

she looked like one of those steely businesswomen you see at the movies, whose buck-chasing husbands have died but are bravely carrying on the Corporation's work themselves, and when she saw me she gave a little squeak of surprise.

'What on earth are you doing here?'

There was no one much about—just a footman bringing in more cases from the hallway—so I explained things as quickly as I could. Luckily she seemed to think it was all a scream, and there was a glint in her eye that told me she was flattered by it—she assumed, you see, that I'd fixed it just to be with her, which I had in a way.

'You won't tell?'

'Of course I won't tell. I think it's perfectly brilliant of you.' She really looked as if she meant it, as well. 'Thank you for the flowers as well,' she said.

'Where's Rasmussen?' I asked, all casual-like.

'Oh he's in the morning room somewhere, looking for Mrs Antrobus.' She flashed me another admiring look. 'Isn't it awful? I've got to spend the afternoon typing letters. But I'll try and get out after tea and we can go for a walk in the park.'

I watched her stride away up the stairs until I realized that the footman with the case was staring at me, but I didn't blame him. She was a looker, you see, and the world stopped when she sailed through it.

*   *   *

Mr Rasmussen was quite at home at Newcome Grange. One or two of the less socially experienced guests, new to the protocols of the country house weekend, sat nervously in their chairs like actors awaiting their cues, but Mr Rasmussen was not among them. He roamed purposefully around the house calibrating his impressions with the photographs he had seen in *Country Life*. He was heard in the servants' hall asking apologetically if he could have the use of a needle and thread. The butler found him in the billiard room admiring the set of Caroline prints that hung there. A county history from the bookcase in the drawing room absorbed him for nearly half an hour.

Mr Rasmussen's interests were strictly interior. On the Saturday morning, when most of the gentlemen went out into the park, he sat in the drawing room and talked to Mrs Antrobus about a mullioned window that ran along one side of the house. 'You see,' he said, 'if you extended the frame by only three or four feet you would enhance what is really a very pretty view down to the river.' And Mrs Antrobus, who had never noticed the window or the view down to the river, thought that he was very good-natured.

On the Saturday afternoon, when an excursion was arranged to a neighbouring estate, Mr Rasmussen said that he had a headache and retired to his room. Clearly it was not a very bad headache, for twenty minutes later he could have been seen— had there been anyone to see him, for most of the servants had been given the afternoon off— walking up the back staircase to the upper floors of the house. Here he looked very interestedly at everything that came his way: at the corridor that led away to the west wing, where there was an antique sundial kept under glass; and at a Marcus Laroon portrait that hung on the wall. Still, anyone who saw Mr Rasmussen—and nobody did—would have said that his interest was not entirely satisfied, that there was something he was in search of that he did not find. He passed an old, glass-fronted bookcase on one of the landings and stopped to look at the books inside it. He tried a door, found it locked and stared hard at it with his hands in his pocket, turning the tips of his shoes thoughtfully on the grey carpet, and was discovered in this attitude by a maid advancing round the corner with a brush and dustpan.

'Can I help you, sir?'

'Do you know,' said Mr Rasmussen, conversationally and with great affability, 'this is such a big house that I declare I have got lost in it. Would that be the bathroom?'

'No, sir. You'll find the bathroom this way. That's the mistress's sitting room.'

Mr Rasmussen apologized for his error and continued on his way.

*   *   *

As for staying at Newcome Grange, I soon found out that it consisted of two basic activities. One of these was eating. The other was hanging about. Seriously. The place was full of bored-looking blokes—the women tended to keep to their rooms—yawning into their handkerchiefs, suggesting a turn round the park or skulking off to the billiard room to play a ludicrous-sounding game called slosh, where you had to run round the table while the balls were in motion. None of this was much in my line, so I tended to sit in one of the downstairs rooms reading the papers, staring out of the windows at the rain and waiting for the gong to summon me back to the dining room, and all the time being on thorns to see if Susie would show.

Actually it wasn't so bad. By this time I'd calculated that the chances of my being shown-up were pretty near zero, and in addition the clergyman, with whom I'd got to be unexpectedly pally, turned out to be a talkative chap who, when he wasn't telling me about his missionary work in the East End, wanted to shoot the breeze about books. By lunchtime on the Saturday he'd even confessed to writing poetry, so I told him to send a file to the *Bugloss* office marked for my—that is, Jimmy's—urgent attention. As for the other guests, Burnage, the comedian, was a frost—simply stood there warming his hands at the fire, eating muffins and looking at the parlour-maids' legs when they bent over to pick up the tea things—and the old women—Lady Llanstephan and Mrs Reginald Heber they were called wouldn't so much as give me the time of day. There were some other people, but the queer thing about country houses, I soon noticed, was that hardly anyone spoke to anyone else. The drawing room after Saturday lunch, with the maids bringing in tea and the butler muttering confidences in Mrs Antrobus's ear—she seemed pleased to see me, at any rate—was like a row of waxworks drawn up on either side of the fireplace.

On the other hand, there were one or two things that did seem to be out of the normal run of country life, or at any rate country life as it's portrayed in those plays where characters in well-cut flannel shorts heave into view every so often hollering: 'Anyone for tennis?' The first was the financial crisis, which hung over the

197

proceedings like a storm-cloud. Every so often, looking out of a window, you'd see a telegraph boy haring up the drive on a bike, and then a few minutes later one of the domestics would advance on a prosperous-looking cove who'd established himself on one of the sofas in the drawing-room, bearing a buff envelope on a salver and he'd rip it open, trying to seem all nonchalant as he did so but actually looking like the chap who gets a letter from the clap clinic on the morning of his wedding. By the Saturday afternoon people were saying that Ramsay Mac had been called back from Chequers the night before and that the country was definitely going off the Gold Standard, and Mrs Reginald Heber sniffed and said it was all red bolshevism and would never have happened in her uncle's time, who I gathered had been some kind of parliamentary under-secretary in Gladstone's last administration.

The second was the presence of Lady Evadne Pargeter. Now, I'm not much of a one for society magazines, but even I'd heard of Lady Evadne, how she'd been painted by Augustus John, danced a Charleston at some party or other wearing only a pair of cami-knickers, and practically driven her elderly father to his grave. She was one of those pale, flighty girls who spend all their time imposing their personalities on the surrounding landscape by talking in a high-pitched voice, ordering cups of tea when everyone else has settled for coffee and generally behaving in a way that a kid of six in a sand-pit would think twice about. In fact, Lady Evadne was worse than this, as she dropped names like a handyman scattering rawl-plugs ('HRH', 'Noel', 'the Beaver'—I think she meant Lord

Beaverbrook) and was, in addition, in a tremendous sulk about something and kept on being summoned to the telephone, from which she returned looking more downcast than ever. She could have given Roper and Hastings a run for their money, too, as she was always plundering the cocktail tray and making surreptitious forays over to the sideboard when she thought no one was looking. There was also a character called Archie someone—a tall, fair-haired chap who talked with a lisp and whose legs looked as if they'd been tied together at the knee with string—with whom she seemed to be getting on particularly badly, and people went about muttering that Evadne was really too *farouche* these days, my dear, and what *must* the Earl be thinking about it.

Actually I had one conversation with Lady Evadne. I was parked on my own in the drawing room reading a copy of *John O'London's Weekly* when she breezed in, saw there was no one else about, looked at me for a moment as if I was Monday's fish, breathed out a great gust of what smelled like *crème de menthe*, and said:

'I say. Do you edit that frightfully clever paper? The *Blue Bugloss*?'

'That's me all right.'

'Then you simply must put in one of Brian's poems. The poor darling says he keeps sending them in, but you just keep ignoring him. Do you know Brian?'

'I'm afraid I haven't had the pleasure.'

'He's really terribly clever. And he'd be most frightfully bucked.'

After that Archie staggered in, so weak at the joints that he looked fit to plunge head-first on the

Axminster, and she gave him a queer look, a bit like Clytemnestra sizing up one of her victims. And that was that.

I won't pretend I didn't enjoy myself, up to a point. When you've been living on pub sandwiches and Lyons fish suppers, decent cooking's not to be sniffed at, not to mention a cushion or two under your bum to help it digest. They didn't stint with the booze either and there were decanters all over the sideboard with the butler standing by to take your order. All the time, though, I could tell that my nerves were whirling round like the carousel at the funfair. There was something odd about Newcome Grange that weekend, what with the financial crisis and Lady Evadne, and you could see that in all sorts of ways, from the footmen tripping over each other in the corridors to the look of black gloom that fell over Mrs Antrobus's face every time she thought no one could see her—the strain was starting to tell. A footman upset a bottle of claret over the table on the Saturday night and I can't have been the only one who thought it looked like blood oozing over the white napiery as Lady Llanstephan practically went into hysterics and had to be calmed down by her maid.

Then, of course, there were the worries that were exclusive to me. On the one hand I knew that I ought to be keeping some sort of eye on Rasmussen, just so that I'd have something to tell Haversham next time I saw him. On the other I'd started worrying about Susie and how much she knew about him. What would she say, I wondered, when she found out—as she was bound to do, the way things were going—that he was supposed to be a crook? As it turned out, keeping tabs on

Rasmussen wasn't a problem. When he wasn't off dictating letters to Susie, which was time I could account for, he simply hung around the place looking at the pictures and soft-soaping the other guests, taking books out of the bookshelves and putting them back and gazing at the furniture rather like an antique dealer who's been given twenty minutes to price a room for a fire sale. If he had his eye on anything in particular, then I didn't see it.

As for Susie, I decided to tackle her about this during our walk in the park. It was the Saturday afternoon and practically everyone else had cleared out to a neighbouring house and tour of his lordship's rose garden or something—even Lady Evadne had been prised away from the drinks tray—and I got out of it merely by making myself scarce when the fleet left. That's always been one of my talents, even back in the days when I was chasing Mrs Bence-Jones and working in the accountant's office at Hove. The rain had stopped and the clouds had gone away somewhere and the ground wasn't too sodden to stop you walking, and so we wandered down the drive a bit and then took a detour round the side of the house where there was a bank of trees and then a kind of lost world of meres and sunken ponds and old birch trees sinking into the ooze that looked as if it'd been there since the dawn of time; it wouldn't have been wonderful to see a pterodactyl taking flight in the direction of the Surrey Hills. Susie was looking completely gorgeous in one of those belted rain macs, with her hair pushed back under a kind of tam o'shanter and a navy-blue scarf that made her face look sort of creamy and inviting against the grey-black surround of the woods and bracken. We weren't getting on too badly, either, and I could see she kept on looking at me in an expectant way, as if she couldn't quite see how things were going to pan out, and in the end, when we'd skirted the lost world and were coming back in sight of the house, I said:

'I heard something about your Mr Rasmussen the other day.'

'Oh yes,' she said casually. 'What did you hear?'

'Oh, somebody said the police were after him or something.'

There was a little spark in her eye as she listened to this that made me think I might've blotted my copybook, but in the end she just laughed.

'That's extraordinary,' she said. 'I never heard anything so funny. Mr Rasmussen of all people! What's he supposed to have done?'

'I don't know.'

'Mr Rasmussen!' she said, still laughing. 'Well I never! Who was it that told you?'

'Just some chap I met in the office.'

I knew that all this stuff about chaps in offices sounded horribly lame and wouldn't bear much cross-questioning.

'They ought to come round and see *me*,' she said, still highly amused. 'I'd tell them something about Mr Rasmussen.'

Above our heads grey sky was crowding in again. The rain would come soon. I could see her struggling to hold back another giggle.

'Never mind about him,' she said. 'You know, I've been thinking about our weekend.'

'Yes.'

'Well, *this* is our weekend, too, isn't it? Here, I got you these.' She was fishing in the pocket of her coat. 'I meant to give them to you before.'

It was a packet of de Reszke, those really classy cigarettes that Beverley Nichols or Noël Coward advertises in the papers. While I was thanking her she said: 'I know you sometimes don't have enough for cigarettes so I thought I'd buy you some.'

That was true enough.

'Go on,' she said. 'Why don't you have one?'

So I smoked one of the de Reszkes, which after the fags I usually smoked was like turning aside from a cheese sandwich to a plate of *pâté de foie gras*, while she hung on my arm and we walked back round the side of the house and peered in at one or two of the windows. There was no one about.

'It's four o'clock,' I said. 'Someone will give us a cup of tea.'

'Actually,' she said, 'I don't know that I want a cup of tea all that much.'

The big hall was empty, with a grandfather clock in the corner chiming the hour and a cat sitting on the staircase watching us as we moved into view. There was a noise of somebody moving about beyond the dining room, but no one came.

'It's all been very odd hasn't it?' she said. 'Meeting the way we did, and you being a writer and that time when . . .' She meant the time Mrs Fanshawe had interrupted the party. She made a vague kind of gesture with her hand and then carefully took off the tam o'shanter.

'I've known them odder,' I said.

With Mrs Bence-Jones it had been the photo albums. With Netta it had been being invited round for a party and finding I was the only guest. The others I couldn't remember. I took her hand and we went up to her room, which was far away in one of the wings of the house. I don't think anything else was said. She had a curious way of looking at me while all this was going on, as if she was lost somewhere in a world where no one else could follow. But what I really remember is the sound of the pigeons in the eaves beyond the window and the wind blowing in against the quivering glass.

I didn't enjoy it much. But then I never do.

*   *   *

Afterwards I lit a cigarette and went and stood by the window, looking out over the park. It was raining quite steadily now and the deer were all hunched up by the fence. In the distance a character in bottle-green gaiters and a check jacket, looking rather like Herne the Hunter, was inspecting what might have been a large pile of cow dung. For some reason my head was full of women's faces: Mrs Bence-Jones, Ethel, Marjorie, the one whose name I couldn't remember that I'd met on the youth-hostelling week, Netta. The funny thing was that I could even hear some of the things they'd said to me; Netta in particular. None of this was calculated to raise my spirits, and as I came back to the bed Susie said:

'Now you're all gloomy.'

'No I'm not.'

'Is it because of me?'

'I don't know what you're talking about.'

'It is because of me, isn't it?'

'Here,' I said, picking up my jacket that I'd thrown on the floor. 'I wrote you this.'

It was that poem I'd been working on. A page and a half long it was, and not half bad, I thought.

'Gracious,' she said. 'I can't read it now. I should be embarrassed. Really I should. But it's terribly sweet of you.'

Beyond the window the gamekeeper—if that's who he was—had stopped looking at the pile of cow dung and was prodding at some moss with his stick.

'I say,' Susie said. Her back gleamed in the light. 'Have you met Lady Evadne Pargeter?'

'I didn't really notice her.'

'Apparently she's a cocaine addict. And she has the most fearful rows with that Archie person.'

'It takes all sorts.'

'You are gloomy.'

A bit later she said: 'I really ought to be going.'

'Do you have to?'

'Oh, but I must. Could you just give me those . . . ? There, on the floor.'

When she'd finished putting her clothes back on, which in some ways was almost as nice as the sight of her taking them off, she said: 'If I don't see you at dinner I'll run out on the terrace afterwards.'

'I'll try and show my appreciation.'

'Whatever happens, we must have lunch on Monday after we get back.'

'I'd like that,' I said.

A bit later I heard her feet scudding along the corridor. It was about a quarter to five and there was no sign of anybody having come back from their trip to the rose garden, so after I'd had another fag I went for a wander through the house. It was all a bit melancholy in the fading light and there was no one about except the butler—a white-haired old boy who couldn't have been less than seventy—who turned up in the dining room, buffing up the underside of a giant epergne with a tin of Silvo. It seemed bad manners to put my head in the doorway without saying anything, so I took a squint at the epergne, which was about two foot high and in the shape of an eagle.

'Tricky job?'

'You can say that again. Dirt gets in the trefoils and then where are you? Sort of thing the mistress notices, too.'

'Mrs Antrobus?'

'That's her.' He lowered his voice a tone or two. 'Between you and me, she's the rummest old bird I ever worked for.'

'Why's she rum then?' He'd clearly marked me down as a kindred spirit, and I thought I might as well get my money's worth.

'Well, always wanting to be drove off all over the place. When she's got a perfectly good house to live in. Raikes—he's the chauffeur—does nothing but ferry her about. And him a married man with children. And then there's the people she has to stay.'

'What's so bad about them?'

'Didn't say there was anything bad about them. Mrs Reginald Heber gave me a ten-shilling note this morning. And very civil of her, too. But that Mr Rasmussen, now, where does he come from? You wouldn't have seen him in a place like this before the war, I can tell you. And Lady Evadne Pargeter, she doesn't know if she's coming or going. Do you know, Albert had to take a bottle of gin up to her room the other night? Nothing left in it either when it came back again this morning. Not to mention the way she takes on at that young man of hers, Lord Harewood's son. There'll be a row tonight, I shouldn't wonder.'

I was hoping he'd say something else about Mr Rasmussen, but nothing came. Just then there was a noise of car doors slamming out on the drive and people began to drift in through the front door, and he started up guiltily and nearly up-ended the tin of Silvo over the table. Somehow I didn't fancy meeting the incoming horde back from their tour of Lord Hogwart's orangery or whatever it was, so I beat a hasty retreat to my bedroom. The women were all crowding through my head again, you see, and what with all the worry of the last couple of days what I really needed was a nap.

All the time I was buoying myself up with the thought that I'd see Susie at dinner, but for some reason, when the time came, there was only Mr Rasmussen, who sat next to Mrs Antrobus and, so far as I could make out, bored her stiff about some antique snuff box or other she owned. No sign of her on the terrace either. Afterwards there were charades or something in the drawing-room, but I thought I'd give them a miss. Instead I went back to my room and read a copy of *A Diary of a Nobody*, which I'd found in the library. When I got bored with that I went and stood by the window, watching the moonlight fall over the park and what looked like blobs of grey cotton wool in the distant fields, which I supposed were haystacks. It had been quite a day, but I didn't know whether I was happier at the end of it than I'd been at the beginning. Outside, the evening noise—servants carrying things about, an almighty crash as somebody dropped a tray of empties—faded away to nothing, and there was one of those long, rural silences, broken only once by the sound of a car of some sort stealing up the drive, and a couple of people whispering on the steps as they got into it. But do you know, I'm such a trusting chap that I never even looked to see who it was.

*   *   *

'But what I really admire about his work is its spaciousness.'

'Yes, that's what I've always liked about it too.'

'That sort of—well—*grandeur* is so rare in contemporary verse, don't you think?'

'Yes it is, isn't it?'

'But of course—I am forgetting—you must be on very familiar terms with him?'

'Actually, he never comes to the office. He just sends the stuff in.'

It was about half-past eleven on the Sunday morning and I was standing on the terrace talking to Rev. Chatterley about F.S. Littlejohn's poems. It had been a funny few hours. When I got down to breakfast the newspapers were full of flaring headlines saying we'd gone off the Gold Standard and there was a picture of Ramsay Macdonald looking like an old hen who's suddenly realized that she's due for the pot. There was no sign of Rasmussen or Susie, but that didn't worry me as most of the guests at Newcome Grange kept strange hours. No one was very talkative, but I gathered from one or two bits of subdued chatter that floated up over the chink of the coffee cups that a couple of events had occurred to disturb Mrs Antrobus's slumber in the wee small hours. For one thing, one of the footmen had been found out cold with concussion after apparently tripping down the back staircase in the dark. For another,

Lady Evadne Pargeter had turned up dead drunk on the carpet outside her room at two o'clock in the morning.

Have you ever had breakfast in a country house? With the kedgeree keeping hot on a little portable heating apparatus on the sideboard and chaps talking about the partridges, and the hostess's friends making catty remarks about whether the marmalade was made by the housekeeper or only bought in from Fortnums? Well, this one was a frost. Either it was the financial crisis, or the thought of Lady Evadne's inroads into the gin, but you never saw such a collection of grim old faces. Plus, I wasn't feeling too good myself. Not because I was especially worried about the Gold Standard, but because I hadn't a clue what Rasmussen might be up to or could think of anything I might say to Haversham the next time he got confidential in the pub. At about half-past nine some of the guests packed off to the village church—you could see the spire half a mile away across the fields—but I skulked off to the library where there was a fire going and a footman eventually brought in a tray of coffee. Those footmen! This one was six feet tall and probably earned more than I did. As he was putting down the tray I said:

'Bad business about that chum of yours.'

'Mackintosh, sir? Rum go if you ask me.'

'Why's that then?'

He looked pleased that I'd asked him.

'Well, sir. Everyone's saying that he fell over his feet in the dark, or was one over the eight, which he may well have been, knowing Sammy. But I was with him when he woke up—nasty crack he'd taken—and he reckoned he'd been pushed.'

'How's that then?'

'Some feller came up behind him he says.'

'Doesn't sound very probable, does it?'

'I suppose not, sir. Will there be anything else?'

Actually there was something else.

'Do you know if Mr Rasmussen has been down to breakfast yet?'

'Left last night sir, I believe.'

'Is that right?'

'Taxi came and fetched him just before midnight.'

Well, that was a bit of a facer all right. Surely if Susie'd known she'd be leaving, she'd have told me? Perhaps she hadn't known. It was all very odd. Anyway, I browsed round the library a bit, which was full of books with titles like *Sermons Preached to a Scots Congregation*, and then sauntered on to the terrace, where the sun had come out and some of the people who'd come back from church were hanging glumly about, and I fell in with Rev. Chatterley.

'And such a welcome relief'—I assumed he was still talking about F.S. Littlejohn's poems, but you can never tell—'from the Sitwell school.'

'You can say that again.'

As to what happened in the next thirty seconds or so (I've gone over it in my head several times), the order of events is unmistakable, for all that my head was full of Susie and Mr Rasmussen and the footman's tumble down the back staircase. First there was a lot of shouting from somewhere above our heads away to the right. Then there was a scuffling noise and the sound of breaking glass. There were heads turning now on the terrace and people staring up to try and work out where the noise came from, which meant that everyone was well-prepared for the third event, which was the sound of an almighty thump as something hit the ground over in the region of the shrubbery.

The Rev. Chatterley's face had gone an uncomfortable shade of duck-egg green. 'What on earth can that have been?' he said.

I could have told him. It was the sound of a body in sharp, irretrievable descent.

*   *   *

Mr Rasmussen got out of the taxi, paid off the driver, watched him slide off in the direction of Old Street and then stood on the pavement looking up and down the City Road. It was eleven o'clock on a Sunday morning—a church clock had just begun to strike the hour—and there was no one much about. The leaves from the trees in Bunhill Fields were strewn all over the road and he put his feet down carefully on them as he walked. A bus came past and he examined the newspaper advertisements on its side. *Alec Waugh's story.* Who was Alec Waugh? For once Mr Rasmussen's intelligence network—infallible when applied to landed estates and dowagers' connections—had failed him. He moved purposefully on over the wet streets, down the steps to his office on the City Road, where there was even more orange peel than ever, and unlocked the basement door. Inside the light had a curious, exhausted quality. A mouse ran suddenly across the carpet and he watched it disappear into a hole in the wainscoting.

An observer—someone who stood in the dimly lit vestibule, say—might have thought that Mr

Rasmussen was bent upon spring-cleaning his office. His first act was to snatch up three or four plaster casts that lay on a desk-top and stow them away in a sack. Then he picked up a sheet or two of cartridge paper, gripped their edges between finger and thumb, set light to them with a cigarette lighter and threw the charring fragments into a wastepaper basket. Some cardboard files, plucked out of a metal cabinet beneath the desk, went the same way. There was an attaché case lying next to the hat-stand, and into this Mr Rasmussen stuffed various documents that he had retrieved from the desk drawers, along with the contents of the cash-box and a quantity of rusty paperclips.

It was surprising how noiselessly Mr Rasmussen went about his work. Once he dropped a paperweight onto the carpet, where it landed with a thump. A few moments later he upset an umbrella that had been dangling from the hat-stand and watched it fall with a look of silent reproach. Then, when he had finished, he lit a cigarette—the sulphur match made a rasping noise as he struck it on the sole of his shoe—and stood smoking it with one foot balanced on the lip of his desk, the smile on his face that of a general summoned at last from temporary quarters behind the front line to the guaranteed comforts of base camp.

*　　　*　　　*

Truth to tell, he hadn't meant to be in the City Road at all. Not that morning anyhow. But somehow the walk back from Hoxton had taken him this way. He was glad to get out of Hoxton. There wasn't anything for him there. Coming down the street with the wind

212

blowing into his unshaven face and nearly taking a tumble on the wet leaves, he felt the bevelled edge of the chisel in his inside pocket banging against his ribs. There might not be ten quid in the Bloke's cash tin, but he'd have something to add to the silver joey, which was all that currently sat on the mantelpiece back in the Caledonian Road. He was so absorbed in the practicalities of his scheme—the chisel worked into the door-frame, a paving stone, if necessary, wrapped up in the cloth in which the chisel nestled—that it took him a moment to realize that the basement door was open. Christ! That was a bit of backsheesh. He could see the Bloke in the grey interior—like a goldfish bowl with all the light making queer patterns—smoking a fag as he put something in a case that lay open on his desk. The Bloke was looking at him. Well, that was fair enough. Daresay he'd look at a feller that came down his area steps on a Sunday morning.

'Oh it's you, Leo,' the Bloke said. He was wearing a rose or something in his buttonhole, a little sprig of red that splashed out of the grey-cloth surround, and smiling. F—— him. 'What can I do for you?'

Suddenly he became aware of the chaos of the room, the charring papers in the bin, the split-open box-files. He had seen this kind of disorder before and knew what it meant.

'I know your game,' he said. 'You're clearing out. That's about the size of it.'

'Really, Leo,' the Bloke said. 'You make me tired. Really you do. What do you want?'

'I want my ten quid,' he heard himself saying. 'That job in Finsbury Pavement.'

The Bloke was still smiling. Funny, now he was

here he didn't want what he'd come for. He'd be just as happy sitting down to a cup of ackamaracka. But that wasn't the way.

'Quite impossible,' he heard the Bloke saying in that toney voice of his. He remembered the woman at the dog track. *O my dear it really is too sweet of you, I must say . . .*

'Ten quid,' he said again, the memory of the woman making him angrier than he'd thought he was. 'Ten quid, you cheesing flat!' He paused again. 'There'll be something to say about that, I reckon. Davenport and Hines now. They could have something to say about that. To the right people.'

'Really, Leo,' the Bloke said. 'This is all quite absurd. No one will say anything.' He had something shiny in his hand. A paperweight, was it, picked up off the floor, a beautiful thing, all blue and green, that the light glinted off peculiarly.

'Ten quid,' he said desperately, getting up on to the balls of his feet, and the chisel banging against his ribs again. He couldn't understand. Ten quid was nothing to the Bloke. Why wouldn't he give it to him? Didn't he know what would happen? Or did he want it that way? His hand was in his jacket pocket now, after the chisel. 'Ten quid,' he said again. 'Or I'm not answerable, see?'

He could never remember who moved first. But the Bloke moved quicker. The chisel was on the floor. How had it got there? There was blood on his fingers. It wasn't the Bloke's, so it must have been his. Losing his temper suddenly he lashed out into thin air, overbalanced and went down heavily on one knee. The Bloke was still smiling, but there were bits of rose petal all over the carpet. His only thought as the paperweight slammed into the side of his face was: *Christ! Who'd have thought the Bloke was up to a dodge like that?* When he came to, there was only himself there, the door flapping in the breeze, the bright blood on his fingers and a little pile of leaves stirring mutinously in the entrance-way. Somewhere in the distance, a clock began to strike the hour.

15

RETURN TO SENDER

Sound Advice for the Salesman: IX. Failure

Remember! There will be times in the career of even the most successful salesman when a situation becomes untenable. No amount of brow-beating will ever convince a customer who simply 'does not want to buy'. It may simply be that, through no fault of your own, you have chosen the wrong time, the wrong place or the wrong product with which to press your suit. Take heart! The prudent salesman does not whine or complain about 'circumstances beyond his control'. He should retire from the scene of operations as gracefully as he can and resolve to 'fight another day'.

Abraxas Salesman's Handbook

Naturally, as soon as they'd retrieved Lady Evadne from among the flowering annuals, all hell broke loose. Within ten minutes the place was an ant-heap of police cars, ambulances, half the women having hysterics and the men all mixing themselves stiff whiskies in the drawing-room. Fact is, I was damned lucky not to end up being called as a witness at the inquest. As it was, Haversham's name did the trick, and after a couple of phone calls to West End Central the village bobby who was interviewing me told me I could sling my hook.

Not, you understand, that I'd seen anything of the slightest interest—I'd been out on the terrace at the time, chewing the fat with Rev. Chatterley and brooding about Susie. Even so, it shook me up, I can tell you, and I spent the rest of the day after I got back to London in no end of a stew. Mostly I was worried about what Jimmy would say if he found out, but then, after a bit, I calmed down and reckoned he'd see the funny side of it. If there was one.

The papers next morning went wall-to-wall about what had happened at Newcome Grange. It turned out that, quite apart from Lady Evadne Pargeter chucking herself head-first over a balustrade and Archie trying to follow suit—he didn't manage it, by the way, and was found blubbering in her bedroom—a couple of portraits by Marcus Laroon had gone AWOL from the upstairs landing. Curiously, though, I hardly noticed. I had my own problems that day, next to which the fatal descent of Lady Evadne was only a sideshow. For a start, when I got to Doughty Street the office was closed up. Or rather there was a small, dark-suited bloke with a face exactly like a crocodile's standing in the hallway eyeing up a big stack of lotion bottles that a couple of workmen were loading up into crates. There was no sign of Hastings.

'What's going on here?' I asked.

216

'Receiver,' says the little bloke, picking up one of the bottles and looking at it doubtfully. 'You owed any money by this concern?'

I thought about it and realized that there was twelve-and-six due from the week before. 'Thirty bob,' I said brightly.

'Work here do you?'

'I'm one of the sales executives.'

'Better put it in writing,' he said, and he handed me a card that said: *Marshall & Lovegrove, Licensed Insolvency Practitioners*, with an address in Cursitor Street. So that was it. Abraxas had gone bust. Seeing the look in my eye, the little bloke went: 'Go on, take half-a-dozen bottles if you like and flog 'em, I shan't mind', but I shook my head. I'd had enough of traipsing around Bayswater and Golders Green telling lies in people's front parlours, and I didn't have the heart.

But this wasn't the last of the day's surprises, not by a long stretch. There'd been that half-arrangement to meet Susie for lunch at the Lyons in City Road, and ten to one saw me in my seat just itching to catch up on the events of the past twenty-four hours. Anyway, one o'clock came, and then one-fifteen, but there was no sign of her, so I decided to drop round at the office and see if she'd been held up. Funnily enough, I could tell as soon as I approached the place that something was up. The light was off in the window beyond the steps, and the door, when I went and tried it, was shut fast. No sign of any coats or hats on the pegs in the vestibule either. I puzzled about this for a good long while, went and stood in the street again, wandered back to the Lyons to see if there'd been some mistake and she'd been there all the time—

there hadn't, and she wasn't and then hung about outside in the street again wondering what to do. After about half an hour I decided that the only alternative plan was to go up to her digs in Kensal Green, so I jumped on a bus and headed north-west through the rain that had come on during the morning, with this terrible sinking feeling cutting me up. There'd been a classical poem I remember having to translate at school about some hero or other who'd had the libation of triumph dashed from his lips at the point of victory: well, that was how I felt crawling up the Harrow Road with the rain lashing the sides of the bus and thin grey light spilling over the greasy pavements.

As I'd half suspected, it was all a frost. The landlady at the digs, who I routed out of her parlour with her hair in curlers, said she'd been gone a month. There was no forwarding address. I don't mind telling you that all this shook me up no end. After all, just a couple of days before we'd been listening to the pigeons clacking under the eaves at Newcome Grange and talking about weekends in the country, and now here she was, to all intents and purposes vanished. Part of me was telling myself to calm down, that there had to be some perfectly decent explanation, but the other part wasn't so sure. I wondered about phoning Haversham—if anyone knew what had happened to Rasmussen it would be him—but the card with his number on it was back at Ma Fanshawe's. Standing on the street corner in Kensal Green, with the rain ruining my collar and the soles of my boots hinting that they weren't made of leather but compressed cardboard, I reckoned that the best thing to do was to take stock. I went off to a cafe in the high street

218

nearby, ordered a cup of tea and a bun and turned out the contents of my pockets on to the formica table-top. There was seventeen bob and a couple of halfpennies, which was a bit of a facer, what with the money owing to Ma Fanshawe and Abraxas going down the pan.

What do you do in such circumstances? In the end I took a bus back to City Road and slunk up to the office again. It was about four o'clock now, with the rain still coming down and the leaves whipping up in spirals round the gates of Bunhill Fields, but would you believe, the light was on down in the area steps and the door was half open. Naturally I breezed down there like a bull elephant expecting to find Susie tethered to her desk and the typewriter going like a Gatling Gun. Instead I bumped smack into Haversham and a couple of coppers who were in the process of unpacking the contents of a filing cabinet on to the roll-top desk. Haversham looked madder than ever—all the skin of his face seemed to be drawn more tightly across the bones than it had been before, like a mask—and when he saw me he said, 'Well, this is a f——g disaster, isn't it?'

'What is?' I asked, thinking the best way of keeping my head above water was to play the innocent.

'Flown the f——g coop,' Haversham said. 'When did you last set eyes on him?'

'Saturday afternoon sometime,' I said, which was the truth.

'Two hundred f——g gramophone sets gone as well,' Haversham said, and I just blinked at him as if he'd been reading the racing results in Chinese. I hung around for a bit, but it was clear that

Haversham had no interest in me. In any case, all the time I was piecing together in my head a version of what had happened, and the more I thought about it the grimmer it got. In the end I went off to the Wheatsheaf, got there just after it opened—it was empty apart from Parkinson, who for the first time in my life I greeted like a long-lost brother and got properly rattled, something I hadn't done for months, and got back to Mrs Fanshawe's with just enough strength in my legs to climb the staircase.

Anyway, next morning when I looked in my wallet there was only two shillings. God knows how many pints I'd stood Parkinson, but it couldn't have been fewer than six. After lunch, when I'd stopped feeling quite so bad, I went out to buy a paper and looked through the commission jobs, but it was all I could do to keep my eye on the page. All the while, too, the thought of what I owed Ma Fanshawe was weighing me down, and even worse than this was the memory of Susie standing in the great hall at Newcome Grange with the tam o'shanter in her hand, and the slow, nervous tramp up the stairs. I've been let down by plenty of girls in the past, you'll understand, but I never thought that Susie would do the dirty on me. It just went to show. All the same, this didn't solve the problem of what I was going to do with myself, not by a long chalk. It was one of those bitter early autumn days when you daren't step out of doors because you know the wind will scrape your chin like a blunt razor, and the clouds are just waiting to explode over your head, as if there was someone up there shouting 'You, you b——r, yes, *you*, you b——r.'

But when it came to it, I knew I had two options: sign on the Labour again, or head down to the old lady's in Tenterden. I didn't fancy either of these above half—the Labour because I've got my pride, like any other working man; Tenterden because the old lady and I never quite hit it off, however hard we tried. In the end, though, I realized there was only one way out. The one and ninepence I had left wouldn't cover the ticket to Tenterden, and I knew I'd need money for expenses, so first I took the evening suit back to the dress-hire shop and got back my half-guinea deposit. The de Reszkes Susie had given me were still in the pocket, would you believe, but do you know I couldn't bring myself to touch them? Then I whisked half-a-dozen books and my second-best shirt down to the pawnshop near Paddington station and raised ten bob on them.

I'd just got back to my room and was tapping the first of the Player's Weights I'd bought with sixpence from the pawnshop money when there was a knock at the door. It didn't sound like Ma Fanshawe, who I wasn't anxious to see just at the moment—she had one of those no-nonsense I'll-see-you-now-my-lad double thumps—so I figured I might as well see who it was.

'Come in.'

What do you know? It was a small, dark-haired woman of about forty—not bad-looking if you liked that sort of thing—who I reckoned I might have seen somewhere before but couldn't quite place. Whoever it was she was clearly in one hell of a state—her eyes had a kind of staring look and the side of her mouth was twitching away like a spring-balance.

'Are you Mr Ross?'

She didn't look like a dun, or anyone to do with

Haversham, so I said: 'Yes, that's me.'

'I'm so glad I've found you . . . It's awful of me to intrude like this.'

'Not at all,' I said, in my toniest voice. I still couldn't for the life of me fathom who she was. 'Won't you sit down?'

'This is terribly embarrassing,' she said. 'Only I've been at my wits' end. Claude used to talk about you, you see, and then I found your name in his address book.'

Just then I twigged. 'You're Mrs Hastings,' I said.

'Yes, that's right. Myra Hastings.' She was looking a bit less flustered now, and I reckoned it would help if I shook her hand. Sure enough she clung to it like Grace Darling and the shipwrecked sailor. 'You see,' she said, 'something absolutely dreadful has happened.'

'You mean, the company going bust?'

'No. It's Claude. I haven't seen him for forty-eight hours. All Saturday morning he was behaving oddly. I thought it was all to do with this trouble at work. You know what he's like, I expect. He always was a sensitive man. But then, after lunch, when I thought we were going for a walk up to Kensal Green cemetery, somewhere a bit quiet that might take him out of himself, he just disappeared. And then, later on, I found a note on the mantelpiece saying that he'd gone away to think things over.'

'I'm very sorry to hear it,' I said, which was the truth now I thought about it. 'Do you have any idea where he might have gone?'

I had a notion that Mrs Hastings was a bit tougher than she looked, as she wheeled out her

222

suggestions as to where Hastings might have skedaddled like the Colonel's daughter when she's been told that the honour of the regiment's at stake.

'It's my belief there's a woman involved,' she said. 'He's not been himself since I can't remember.'

Funny, that afternoon at the Pegasus Club had only been five days ago, but it seemed like an eternity. I had no trouble in guessing who the woman was. Where would they be now, I wondered? Marjorie liked weekends in Weymouth. Or, failing that, Southend. But Hastings! It just goes to show what these solid, suburban types are capable of when they're pushed. I wondered whether to tell Mrs Hastings—the daughter of the regiment look had gone now and she was sniffing into a lace-edged handkerchief—about Marjorie and the Pegasus Club. Somehow, it didn't seem like a good idea.

'Mrs Hastings,' I said. 'I think it's quite possible that Claude—Mr Hastings—is under quite a lot of psychological strain at the moment. He may simply have decided that what he needs is a period of calm reflection.' She looked a bit doubtful at this, so I breezed on: 'He's always told me how devoted he is to you. I'm sure you'll find that there's a perfectly reasonable explanation.'

If I knew the perfectly reasonable explanation, she'd be at the Weymouth Imperial by now, leading Hastings one hell of a dance, but it's what women like to hear. Anyway, it seemed to cheer up Mrs Hastings no end, and she stuffed the handkerchief into the sleeve of her coat and said:

'Perhaps you're right. I'm very sorry to have

223

disturbed you, Mr Ross.'

'Not at all, Mrs Hastings.'

'And if you should hear anything you'll let me know? Flaxman 272.'

'Of course.'

And then she was gone, down Mrs Fanshawe's rickety staircase, leaving me with my upturned suitcase and the pile of books.

*   *   *

There's a poet somewhere who talks about the contents of a room stirring up a host of pleasant associations of a life well-lived, but it wasn't how mine looked just at the moment. Fact is, it looked like a bomb-site recently inhabited by a derelict who'd been living off stale bread crusts. In the end I packed everything I'd got bar some old poetry magazines—the next occupant was welcome to them—into a suitcase, took a last look round the place (oddly enough, the thing I remembered was Susie talking to Ma Fanshawe with the brassiere she'd forgotten to put back on lying incriminatingly under the chair) and marched off down the stairs. The trick if you're doing a flit—and I've done several—is to act nonchalant and make anyone looking believe that you're just off round the corner for a packet of aspirin. As it happened, I'd no sooner got to the hallway when I bumped into Mrs Fanshawe's brother, but I flung back my shoulders and gave him a 'Good afternoon!' of such paralysing heartiness that he simply stared at me and even held the door open to let me out. Ten minutes later I was sitting on a bus heading south in the direction of Charing Cross with all the stuff from the last three

224

days boiling up in my head: Lady Evadne Pargeter (there was a paper on the seat with a headline that read SOCIETY GIRL'S TRAGIC FALL—nobody had liked to say it was suicide); Haversham in the basement office; and Susie lying invitingly across the bed with her legs curled up against her stomach at Newcome Grange as the pigeons clacked in the eaves. Especially Susie.

As the train went south through the Kentish countryside, it struck me that several things in my life had all come to an end at the same time. Well, that wasn't so bad was it? It was when things filtered out inconclusively that you got trouble. I wondered what Mrs Hastings would say to Hastings when she saw him again. He'd go back to her in the end, all right. They always did. Marjorie was a grand girl, but no one with all their faculties present would stay with her longer than a week. Expensive, too. They were finishing off the harvest in the wheat fields outside Tonbridge, and I looked out of the window at the farm labourers out cutting hay stooks, running in rows across the stubble, and thought about a couple of weeks' hop-picking I'd once done there back in the distant days when there didn't seem so much to worry about: cockney voices, hop-bines smouldering under the tea-kettles and the smell of the juice trickling over your fingers, which is deuced difficult to get off. Then the wheat fields started to give way to pasture, a house came in sight close up to the track, you could see the church spires in the near distance, and I got that sinking feeling in the pit of my stomach made up of a series of remembrances of stucco house-fronts, the perfume-stink of Earl Grey tea, Cairn terriers, bridge fours, the novels of Hugh Walpole, gas-fires cranked up to 'stun', jars of barley-sugar and the old lady standing vigilant before her hearth.

Actually it's not so bad here in Tenterden. The old lady's calmed down a bit in the two years since I was last this way and now she's given up the hay-box cookery the food's definitely middling-to-good. There are worse things to do with your time, after all, than to sit by the fire with a couple of fat cushions under you to take the strain and look at the mist while someone makes you a cup of tea and asks: will you have a chocolate biscuit or plain? Jimmy was as good as his word, too, and took some poems, so at least there's pocket-money. The *Blue Bugloss* pays its contributors with Coutts & Co. cheques, which impresses the old lady no end. There was even a copy of it left out on the parlour table the other week when a couple of her cronies came round for tea.

The rest of the past couple of months didn't stop knocking at the door either. Queerly enough, I came across Rasmussen's photograph in *Police News* again the other day, with a full account of what he was wanted for. Never mind those two Marcus Laroons gone from the upstairs landing, and the other stuff. Apparently he'd sold 200 gramophones at the shop in High Holborn without any of the suppliers twigging that it was a long-firm fiddle, whereby you scarper with the proceeds before settling your debts. All this set me thinking about Susie again, and how she'd pulled the wool over my eyes—if she really had pulled the wool, which I wasn't sure about—but in the end I thought, good luck to her. You have to take the rough with the smooth where women are concerned, at least that's always been my experience.

226

And, even queerer than seeing Rasmussen's picture in *Police News*, I got a card from Netta. I've no idea how she knew my whereabouts, and I half-suspected the old lady had a hand in it, but there it was—nothing about the vow she'd taken never to speak to me again and the engagement ring she'd chucked at me in the cinema queue that time, and instead some stuff about books she'd been reading and a married cousin of hers in the vicinity she'd be coming to visit, and might we meet up.

Might we? I don't know. The letters on the old lady's mantelpiece, together with the complimentary copies of the *Blue Bugloss* and the Tenterden Trefoil Guild's winter programme. What with them and the rain, the terrible English rain that falls day and night without cease, I think I've got enough to be going on with for the moment, thank you very much.

16

ENVOI

Sharply the menacing wind sweeps over
The tattered winding sheet of the day.
The banker broods on the train to Dover
While the skivvy plods her homeward way.
An instalment plan for the Drage's sofa
Sits on the chair near the aspidistra
The Hoxton Jew and the West End loafer
Gaze at the cloud that's as black as bistre
I was taught to believe in a better age
That had been before and would come again
Settled instead for a living wage
An English sky, and English rain.

James Ross—'Autumn Meditation',
New English Review, *December 1931*

Beyond Greenwich the channels grew freer of shipping and it was possible for the boat to move out into the rough water of the Blackwall Reach. It was raining quite hard and there was a clump of barrels lying in the middle of the deck that had not been properly secured and kept clanking together. The Kentish coastline, which shortly after this became visible through the murk, seemed faintly unreal, like badly painted theatrical scenery that men in white coats and aprons might soon come and start dismantling. Mr Rasmussen sat on a small bench in the lea of the foc'sle, where there was much less wind than might have been expected and

228

the smoke from his cigar helped to dissipate the smell of the coconut oil. He said:

'Well, here we are. Beggars can't be choosers. That is what I always say.'

'I don't know about beggars,' Miss Chamberlain said. She was wearing an expensive-looking fur coat buttoned up to the neck and sat at the far end of the bench. 'I think it's a very nice boat.'

'That is because you have never travelled anywhere,' said Mr Rasmussen sententiously. There was a white gauze bandage wound around his wrist and he scratched at it with his forefinger. 'When you have made as many journeys as me, you will know that there are ships and ships. Ships and ships,' he said again. 'And salt water beneath them.'

We have lingered in the chambers of the sea
By sea-girls wreathed with seaweed red and brown
Till human voices wake us, and we drown.

'Is that something from one of Cochran's revues?' Miss Chamberlain asked. The boat flew the flag of one of the new Baltic states and all three of the ships' officers had asked her if she would be at dinner that evening so that she might hear them sing.

Mr Rasmussen did not reply. There was a briefcase lying on the bench at his side and he picked it up and placed it fondly in his lap. Then he said, 'I think I shall go into politics. That is the thing to do now. There is no money to be made in business any more.'

For some reason Miss Chamberlain seemed to find this very funny. When she had finished laughing she said, 'But think of all the banquets you would have to attend and all the disagreeable people you would have to sit next to. You always say that disagreeable people are the bane of your life.'

The smell of the coconut oil had almost disappeared by now, to be replaced by a distinct odour of rotting fish. Mr Rasmussen wondered whether to smoke another cigar but then thought better of it. The rain, which had lessened slightly as they chugged past Thamesmead and Erith, was now coming down even harder.

'These things are always a wrench,' he said.

'I'm sure you're right.'

'But then most of our lives are spent casting off some association or another.'

'I suppose they are.'

'Taking leave of places and so forth.'

'I'm sure I read that in a book somewhere.'

'I shouldn't dream of correcting you.'

'We really ought to go and have lunch,' Miss Chamberlain said briskly. 'The captain told me he had at least four kinds of pickled herring he wanted us to try.' Her fingers, fossicking in the pocket of her coat, came upon a piece of paper with thick, irregular handwriting on the topmost side and she took it out and examined it for a moment.

'What's that you have there?' Mr Rasmussen asked without much interest.

'Nothing,' Miss Chamberlain said, a shade less briskly. She looked for a moment as if she might put the piece of paper back in the pocket of her coat, but then changed her mind and in a sharp, decisive gesture cast it over the side.

'Well then,' Mr Rasmussen said, following the

movement of her arm appreciatively. Out in the channels the blue-green water boiled furiously. A moment or two later they went below.

Acknowledgements

Thanks to David Kynaston, J M-R, J.C. and Andreas Campomar.